Living with Snakes

WITHDRAWN
UTSA LIBRARIES

Winner of

THE FLANNERY O'CONNOR AWARD
FOR SHORT FICTION

Living with Snakes

Stories by Daniel Curley

The University of Georgia Press
Athens

© 1985 by Daniel Curley
Published by the University of Georgia Press
Athens, Georgia 30602
All rights reserved

Set in Linotron 202 Baskerville
The paper in this book meets the guidelines for
permanence and durability of the Committee on
Production Guidelines for Book Longevity of the
Council on Library Resources.

Printed in the United States of America

90 89 88 87 86 85   6 5 4 3 2 1

Library of Congress Cataloging in Publication Data
Curley, Daniel.
    Living with snakes.

    Contents: Trinity—The inlet—The other two—
[etc.]
    I. Title.
PS3553.U65L5   1985   813'.54   84-22773
ISBN 0-8203-0767-X

"The First Baseman" originally appeared in the
Cimarron Review and is reprinted here with the
permission of the Board of Regents for Oklahoma
State University, holders of the copyright.

TO AUDREY

Acknowledgments

The author and the publisher gratefully acknowledge the magazines in which stories in this volume first appeared.

New Letters: "Trinity" and "The Contrivance"
New England Review: "Wild Geese"
Story Quarterly: "Reflections in the Ice" and "Living with Snakes"
Cimarron Review: "The First Baseman"
Chicago: "The Inlet"
Quarterly West: "Billy Will's Song"
Mid-American Review: "Visiting the Dead"
Another Chicago Magazine: "The Other Two"

Contents

Trinity

And then the Andersons met again at the deathbed of their child. Theirs had been a particularly vicious divorce. Every item of property had been the subject of separate and distinct acrimony, each book in the bookcase, each stick in the woodbin, each plastic spoon in the picnic basket. Their lawyers hated them. The judge contemned them and, being merely a human judge, arranged everything with absolute impartiality, the settlement best calculated to infuriate both sides. He arranged custody of the child with a miracle of checks and balances that would have tried the patience of saints. A Solomon would have seen at once that the only thing to do was divide the child. Even then, venom would have flowed over how it was to be done, lengthwise or across.

It must be clearly understood that the death was something for which neither could blame the other. There had been no carelessness, no oversight, no omission on either hand. Nor had the child taken it on herself to punish her parents by sudden death, by happy accident, real or feigned, or by the slow torment of anorexia. No, she was a perfectly happy child of divorce who simply chanced to sicken and die at her summer camp.

He—Lars Anderson—came back from walking in the Highlands. She—Dolores Anderson, nee Sanchez y Silvera—came back from skiing in New Zealand. For five days they faced each other across the child, listening to each heavy breath as if it were the last and to be remembered always. Long before the end they prayed an earnest prayer of no faith for a miracle, for life or death, for release for all of them.

The silence when it came was worse than the labored finality of each breath. There was now nothing to listen to but each other. She heard him say, "Are you all right?" He heard her say, "Can you stand it?" Of course they were neither of them all right. They could neither of them stand it. They leaned on each other out of the room and down the corridor and into the elevator.

In the privacy of the elevator she confessed, "I blame myself."

"You mustn't," he said. He was quickly estimating the value of a similar confession on his part, but he didn't want to get into a fight over who had the greater sense of guilt. He didn't want to start up old times.

He was still debating within himself when the elevator stopped at the next lower floor. They sprang apart as if they had been seizing a moment of desperate love. The door opened and a priest strode in. He was red-faced and gray and smelled of after-shave and deodorant—or perhaps that was the flowers he was carrying. He made them feel disgusting after their long vigil, as if he were seeing in their clothes and in their eyes the true state of their souls.

The priest addressed himself to the control panel of the elevator, but with a bowl of flowers in each hand he was unable to manage the button. He gestured his helplessness with the bowls, with his shoulders, with his head, with a helpless smile. "Will you please punch Two for me?" he said.

"Oh," Lars said, "sorry." And while he was saying it, Dolores pushed the button, barely in time.

The priest began his charge out of the elevator. "Have a good day," he said, managing to add no priestly overtones to the cliché. He looked at neither of them.

"It's not likely," Lars said.

"Our child has just died," Dolores said.

The priest was now out of the elevator. "I'll pray for him," he said without pausing or turning around.

"I'd rather you didn't," Dolores said.

"We don't believe," Lars said.

"We're all the same in God's eyes," the priest said out of the middle of his striding back.

The doors closed. Lars and Dolores fell into each other's arms. It was suddenly real.

That night at Dolores's motel they comforted each other as best they could. Mute despair led to half words. Half words led to tentative pats. Pats led to caresses. Caresses led to embraces. And embraces led to the blind old pantomime of denying death, futile and forever hopeful. They fell asleep to Do you remember? and Do you remember? They woke to a dream of remembering. Dolores remembered First Tooth, First Step, First Word. What Lars remembered chiefly was that earnest hand clutching his forefinger as they walked on Sunday morning through the zoo, communing with the beasts, their careful substitute for Mass.

"We never did find our totem animal," he said.

"It might have helped," she said.

"Please don't start that," he said, retreating all the way to comforting pats—but no further.

"Sorry," she said.

But each lay in the dark and reviewed the dim, massive, fierce shapes in an endless frieze: the hopelessly large and the unimaginably small, mammoth and amoeba, saber-toothed tiger and midget shrew, blue whale and plankton, all raging with assertive life. Lars and Dolores still had the rest of their lives to choose, although the choice was no longer important. They didn't really want to know where they had gone wrong.

"What it comes to," he said, "is that there is no one else, anywhere on earth, who can remember with me."

"Yes," she said. Although her answer was undoubtedly the right one, he had a sense he was talking to a star which might already have been extinct for a thousand years before this present light reached the earth. But that light, he knew, was all he had.

And it was by this light that they decided—no, they decided nothing. They followed the light without knowing or really caring if it was a Star in the East or the very ignis fatuus. They found themselves together again in the old house, which Dolores had never left. The gaps in the bookcase were plugged. The woodbin was replenished. The picnic basket once again had its full complement of spoons. All was as it had been, although everything was different.

Together they burned their child's clothes, her books, her games, and all that was hers. But they made a strict calculation of the value and gave that sum, anonymously, to Goodwill Industries.

"We must keep her picture," Dolores said.

"But not by our bed," Lars said.

"Nor yet isolated as a shrine," Dolores said.

"No," Lars said.

But a shrine was exactly what it did become. No matter how it was moved, from the piano to the bookcase, to an ancient sideboard, it managed to attract bowls of flowers. Its flat metal art deco frame picked up glints of distant candles. It was a focus of gravity and bent Lars and Dolores's straightest lines into orbits (not that at this time any of their lines were particularly straight).

They found themselves on Sunday mornings retracing their steps in the zoo. They would bring the Sunday papers and sit on a bench upwind of the bears. They had never before noticed the number of parents with children and were surprised because they used to think their solution to the Sunday problem was unique. Now it was clear there were others who couldn't leave Sunday to chance, who needed some dodge, both for the children and themselves.

"For a dodge it's not too bad," Dolores said.

"Better than most," Lars said.

"Name one," Dolores said. There were many things besides Sunday that Dolores was not able to leave alone. In fact, her abstract love of debate was, in Lars's eyes, one of the main reasons their marriage became a shambles. She would demand reasons and then reject them. She would demand better reasons and supply them herself while he was still in shock from her barrage. Her better reasons were usually revolting.

"The zoo was better for us anyway," Lars said. He tended to get stuck on a point that had seemed safe, and safety was what he mainly required. And when he had been bombed out of his shelter and didn't know where to run, when he had no better and better reasons, he was as like as not to smash plates, slowly, deliberately, and without apparent anger. She charged him for the plates in their monthly reckoning, and he was glad to pay for what seemed to him the only adequate rebuttal to her reasons.

"Go on," Dolores said. "Name one."

"As a Sunday dodge," Lars said, "the zoo is better than the Unitarian church." He had been brought up a Unitarian and endlessly resented it.

"And why is that?" she said. This was an old routine. She could take him through more steps than this before he set fire to the paper.

"Unitarianism, like decaffeinated coffee, leads to schizophrenia," he said. He was proud of that. He had lain long awake polishing the epigram. He was ready for her.

"Aha," she said. She was astonished but relentless. "And why is that?"

He had not polished that far, but he had an uncut gem or two he hoped would pass. "The pursuit of form while denying the essence," he said. "The compartmentalized mind." He had run through his hoard and said with only apparent irrelevance, " 'I think I could turn and live with animals.' "

"That's bullshit Walt Whitman," she said. The literary game had always been one of their standbys. It helped disguise the fact that they didn't like each other.

" 'A thousand types are gone,' " he said.

"Tennyson—Tennyson," she said. "*In Memoriam*— 'So careful of the type, but, no, a thousand types are gone' blah blah." He was drawing her away from the fight, but she didn't care. Sometimes if he caught her soon enough she didn't care, was glad even. She could never remember why the peacemakers were blessed, but she knew they were— except when they were bastards.

" 'Some keep the Sabbath going to church,' " she said. "How about that?"

"Emily Dickinson," he said piously.

"Cutesy Emily," she said. "What a dimwit. You know, Emily Merton told me that when she was a child she was converted to Ornithology one Sunday morning in that very birdhouse. A man said 'Tyranus tyranus,' and her life was changed." She gestured across the shaded lawn toward the aviary, which they could not see but which they both faced as infallibly as if it had been Mecca.

At once, without a word or a glance exchanged, they got up and began to cross the lawn, abandoning the *Times* to the wind, which riffled the pages impatiently and strewed the sheets about as if the news were very bad indeed. They entered the aviary through the double, bird-proof doors, accompanied by an upwardly mobile sparrow.

The vast interior was shrill with the cries of birds. Other than that it was hot and wet and still. Only the sweep of wings and the flash of color showed what was really there, although the jungle foliage was boiling with life and the very air was fraught with fecundity. Cautiously Lars and Dolores patrolled the limits of the jungle, which was held at bay only by a low glass fence. Gross cockatoos hung from the branches. Gaudy flamingos dozed on one foot in the pools. Lars and Dolores peered into the undergrowth for the hidden birds, caring only for the most secret.

Lars—a word man after all—found himself reading the descriptive cards attached to the fence. "*Mimus polyglottos polyglottos,*" he murmured. "*Ardea herodias.*" He saw Dolores's lips moving as if in prayer.

"*Vermivora peregrina,*" she was saying. "*Megaceryle alcyon alcyon.*"

Once, as he muttered, "*Bombycilla cedorum,*" Lars caught his breath at the rush of wings beside his ear and the sudden appearance out of nowhere of a glorious gem on a branch not a foot from his face. But it was only a hummingbird. The godhead of Ornithology chose not to reveal itself. Lars studied the cards and found the hummingbird. "*Archilochus colubris,*" he said firmly. "Lovely," he added.

Then, on the edge of despair, he drew himself up and said magnificently, "*Riparia riparia riparia,* thrice."

"Perhaps we're too old," Dolores said.

"I never did learn to pronounce Latin," Lars said. "The teacher was only a day ahead of us on the grammar."

"How do you know that?" Dolores said. She didn't intend to start anything, but even here, in the very heart of the jungle, her old reflexes were still in command.

"The teacher was my mother," Lars said as if the question were simply polite. "We did our homework together on the dining room table."

At this time they went to bed each night—and some afternoons—with the greed of newlyweds. They forced skin against skin in hope of a total penetration, trying to drive skin into skin, to mingle their blood, to achieve a more-than-Siamese union. What they wanted was no less than the total permeation of the Trinity. But they succeeded only in mingling sweat. Their surfaces slipped over each other with the long moan of a stone skimming across the ice. They fell asleep to "I remember" and "I remember" and woke to a sense of growing desolation.

The photograph in its art deco frame continued to prowl the room, turning three times around on the mantelpiece before settling darkly down. Even there, however, it contrived to catch the flicker of firelight from a distant mirror. And when it nestled in a corner of the window ledge, the lights of wandering cars caused it to flare out in the night like an alarm.

They never knew what they wanted, but they were not out of touch with their feelings. In fact, their feelings tormented them incessantly. They just didn't know what these feelings commanded. They didn't know if they were to spring at each other's throats or move soundlessly apart or continue in despair, noisy or mute. A child was to be the sign, and there was no child. A child was to be the sign, but Dolores's body refused the penance her mind would impose. Once when her period was three days late they looked at each other in growing horror and saw that their punishment was greater than they could bear.

"It's a second chance," Lars said hopefully, as a battered soul might receive a sentence of ninety-nine half-lives in Purgatory.

"A second chance," Dolores said, "to do the only thing we know how to do: fuck up."

"You don't think we've learned anything?" Lars said.

"A.," Dolores said, even now in full command of her rhetoric, "A., if you mean have we learned something about our capabilities, I think we have, and B., if you mean have we learned how to apply our knowledge for constructive ends, I think we have not."

"I think so, too," Lars said, although actually he had thought nothing of the kind, no matter how deeply he had felt it.

They watched with dismay as the head of their child was turned into the red and swollen moon, half-hidden, half-revealed by the veils of the window-ledge shrine. They knew then that the decision had been taken out of their hands and that they were free once more in their determined fate.

"Bosh," the doctor said. He was a very clever doctor and could speak more Latin than any aviary, but he had to get up his small talk out of Victorian novels where most things are not talked of at all. "Bosh," he said and put an end to the whole idea of her pregnancy. "You must be very anxious." He knew all about them and knew what cause they had to be anxious—or at least he knew as little about them as anybody else who knew all about them. "It will take care of itself in time."

But taking care of itself is exactly what it did not do, nor did it take care of them. They were right back where they started—or farther. Their fate had not accepted them, and now, knowing the awfulness of that fate, they could judge the worse depths to which they had plunged. Still, they kept to such routines as they could contrive. They read their books. They lit their fires. They piously carried their picnic basket into the woods, always avoiding that one spoon exuberantly marked with the prints of tiny teeth.

In a little known park they had their favorite picnic table in a glade few people found, and none at a time when Lars and Dolores were there. Sometimes there were cold ashes in the grill, careful trash in the barrels, but no other sign. They sat side by side with a view, leaf-fringed, over a little pond where kingfishers swooped and dived. They dealt curiously with a familiar raccoon that hung under the edge of their table and found food on top like a magnet sensing a needle even through wood. For the local birds they crumbed more bread than they themselves ate, and they forgot, for the time, that they were cursed and that they didn't like each other.

"Gray-cheeked thrush," Dolores said. They sat side by side with their binoculars focused on an obscure bird rattling among the fallen leaves.

"Olive-backed," Lars said, perhaps incautiously, for the bird flew on into the deep woods.

"Perhaps," they agreed, conceded.

"The horses play in the field," Dolores said suddenly. "A child is swinging."

"That's not literary," Lars said. He felt as if she were breaking some rule, ignoring the umpire's call, or sending forbidden signals in charades.

"I never said it was," Dolores said.

"It's what you said after you fainted at the hospital," Lars said.

"They thought I was crazy," Dolores said.

That was the first day at the hospital when the doctors told them it was only a matter of time. Dolores fainted— perhaps partly from jet lag—after all, New Zealand. She opened her eyes and said, "Horses," said, "Child." She kept on saying it until she slept, and they had indeed thought she was crazy. Lars had seen the looks they exchanged, doctors, nurses, aides, even the woman mopping the tiles outside the door.

They all looked at her and nodded their heads and said, "Horses," said, "Child," while they listened to her heart and examined her eyes. Lars, too, nodded and thought, Horses, thought, Child.

"Do you know what I meant?" Dolores said.

"Yes," Lars said.

"Did you know immediately?"

"Yes," Lars said.

"Did you think I was crazy?"

Lars said, "No." But he knew he had hung fire. She accepted his answer, however, and they looked at each other strangely and shared a summer's day at a country school in Maine, a picnic table under some trees, horses running in the surrounding field, and a child—unnamed—swinging joyfully in the deserted schoolyard.

But in spite of this moment shared, doubts grew. Had Lars really understood at once? Was Dolores really crazed by grief? The doubts, however, were of self. It was Dolores who feared she might have been driven distracted, and Lars who remembered a blinding flash of blank when Dolores first spoke. The blank perhaps could not have been measured in time, but it was clearly there. And Dolores's mind had made a leap not normally available to the waking, healthy mind.

"It's a question of what we owe ourselves," Dolores said. She rolled off Lars with a sound like adhesive tape pulling loose. Although they no longer believed, they went through the motions of creation.

"I suppose," Lars said, "we owe ourselves whatever we owe her." He didn't know what he meant, but it was minimally comforting.

"That's true enough," Dolores said, "as far as *we* goes, but I mean *I* and I mean *you*."

Lars glanced through the open door into the living room, but the picture was dark. By the simple act of moving it to the other side of the window ledge, they had deprived it of all light—candle, fire, car, moon. "I don't know what I owe you," he said, "and I don't like to think you owe me anything at all."

"I mean, what I owe myself and what you owe yourself," Dolores said, twisting Lars's undershirt about her loins.

"Oh," Lars said. He had never thought of that, his deepest assumption, and it still cast no light at all on what Dolores had called constructive ends. But it opened a gap through which they slipped. They got out of bed—each on his proper side—and went their ways without any plan, constructive or not.

However, sometimes in the cold high places—Lars had taken to exploring Machu Picchu—or in the heart of the sea—Dolores had gone in for skin diving—fingering the texture of carven stone or rapt before bright fish among the ribs of ancient wrecks, they felt a rush by their ears, an immanence.

The Inlet

Kiner rowed easily and well, but the wind out on the lake was very strong. The light aluminum boat went more sideways than ahead in spite of all he could do to keep it lined up with the mountain ash just over Judith's left shoulder. He looked behind him to see where he was. There were two anchored boats of fishermen he had to avoid and the place where the ducks seemed to be standing on something just submerged.

He rounded the point where the man had told them eagles were nesting. It really didn't look at all a likely place. The man's gesture had been vague, however, and there were other points, more remote, more likely. But the next one was a long way off, at least a mile across the open bay, twice that if he tried to stay in the shelter of the shore.

"Move a little to the left," he said.

She moved a very little, but he felt the balance of the boat shift. He shifted fractionally himself to achieve some pure ideal of his inner ear. He thought of his hands. He had expected blisters, but he didn't feel them yet, although he was afraid to look. It had been a long time since he had rowed. He selected a new landmark, a flagpole growing right out of the top of her head. It looked like a Martian antenna, especially with the great goggle-eyed field glasses she was using at the moment.

"UFO's?" he said.

"Ducks," she said.

"What kind?"

"Standard mottled brown," she said.

"That eliminates a lot," he said.

"And leaves a lot," she said.

"The waxwings were nice," he said. The mountain ash had been full of waxwings when they passed.

"Waxwings are always nice," she said. Her emphasis was on *always*. She wasn't giving an inch.

"So was the kingfisher."

"Yes," she said. She lowered the glasses. "The light is all wrong."

The kingfisher had patrolled back and forth beside them as he labored to round a particularly windy point. It fell from a tree and screamed and dived and skimmed the water. Then it shot upward toward a dead overhanging limb, slowed, and stalled just on the limb.

"I need a new bird," she said. "A new place, a new bird for my life list."

"Maybe we'll see the eagle," he said.

"I've seen an eagle," she said.

But he hadn't and he was hopeful. He checked behind him and decided to cut across the bay, not directly to the eagle point, by any means, but still to a spot that would cut off a very considerable corner. He thought he saw an inlet there. Perhaps not. But it was something to aim for. His landmark was now two pine trees. Her head rested just between them. They were like her big earrings.

"Where did you see the eagle?" he said.

"Oh, in Canada," she said, offering just that much of her history. It was like being in an elevator. The door opens. Seventh floor, camping supplies. The door closes. She didn't look up. She had her Peterson open to a page of ducks. He knew it well, all the mottled browns.

"Probably mallards," he said.

"Probably," she said.

"Or black or gadwall or mottled or pintail—oh, those mysterious females."

She looked at him then. It took an effort not to, seated as they were. "Not mottled," she said, "not here." She always knew more about birds than he did.

The wind was blowing him too close to one of the fishing boats, so he turned directly upwind and gave up all landmarks. "Are you warm enough?" he said. He had taken off his jacket and it was lying beside her.

"Oh, yes," she said. She picked up her glasses and scanned the nearest shoreline. He had to smile and nod to the men in the boat. They silently raised their beer cans to him.

The other boat was anchored near the inlet he was aiming for. He saw that she was discreetly studying it over his shoulder. The great lenses of her binoculars were just off his face. If it hadn't been for them, he might have thought she was looking at him. He wondered what she had been thinking when he had that flagpole in the middle of her head.

"It's them," she said.

He hesitated a moment, wondering if he was going to be stupid. "Them?" he said.

"From the lodge." Her tone implied that he was stupid. "The woman with muscular dystrophy or MS or whatever."

"Them," he said. They had seen the husband carry her on his back down the long steps to the lake. The little girl carried her purse. The boy carried cushions.

"That's devotion," Judith had said at the time.

And he had said, " '. . . did on his back the old Anchises bear.' You don't see that sort of thing every day."

"You bore for twenty-five years," Judith said. "I bore for fifteen. So what else is new?"

"But not like that," he said.

"It was worse," Judith said.

She was right. It was worse. Much longer than this was likely to be and much worse. At least the woman had her arms around the man while they were going down the steps. Kiner himself had felt on his back only the weight of a house and mortgage. And now he was bearing again. She was bearing. Bearing each other, bearing—worse, far worse—themselves. All those years all over again.

"He won't leave her," Judith said. "She's sure of him."

Kiner kept well clear of the fishers in the boat and came to the inlet. "I'm going to rest here for a bit," he said.

"We don't have to go on," Judith said.

"I just want to rest out of the wind," he said.

"I can row," she said.

"Of course you can," he said, "but rowing is a passion with me."

"I'm glad to know what is," she said.

The entrance to the inlet was blocked partially with weeds and partially with a fallen tree, but he maneuvered the boat in, rowing some, poling some, pushing off from the fallen tree and tangling with the weeds.

Once they were really off the lake, everything was still. There was no wind. There was no perceptible current. The water was dull and black. Nothing stirred on the low, level banks.

"It's a swamp," he said. And he felt a desire to follow the sluggish stream up into the land, winding, turning, turning perhaps all the way to the eagles.

"Reminds me of the Everglades," she said.

He waited. But there was nothing further: Eighth floor, alligator purses, egret plumes, fur coats, and wampum. He had to make an effort. "I went through the Everglades once," he said.

"You told me," she said.

He must have told her a lot that first night they had slept together, told all the first-night things, told I, I, I, this is who I am. Who you are holding.

"I know," she said.

Having gone so far, however, he said, "It was at night. Great birds flopped off the road. The dark was full of eyes. It was very cold."

"And you slept shivering and alone in a whorehouse in Tampa," she said.

"I guess I did," he said. "Shall we explore?"

She shrugged. With her glasses she was exploring the undergrowth on the banks.

He soon found in the twisting and cramped quarters of the stream that he had to look over his shoulder all the time, so he decided to row backward. He pivoted the boat—not quite without effort. He had to think deliberately: pull on the left oar, backwater on the right. It was a little like patting his head and rubbing his stomach.

"That was neat," she said.

He didn't want to presume. She still might be forgiving nothing. "Thank you," he said.

"So easy," she said.

He wished it had been harder, that he had had to think more, had to fight his muscles, scream at them, beat them with whips. It had been hard to learn, of course, but quite painless to resurrect.

"Where did you learn it?" she said.

"I guess I've always known it," he said. "There were always boats."

Where did he learn it actually? He would like to remember that he had learned it when he and his father were fishing, but his father had always rowed. He himself was too little then. Or it might have been those later Saturdays when he had rowed his mother's friend the fat cop. Very likely. He had had plenty of time then to think how to do it, what to tell his arms to do. He didn't even take a fishing pole then because it was understood that he liked to row and the cop liked to fish. A perfect relationship. Why, his mother even bought a pair of pajamas and gave him the bottoms and the cop the top because that's the way they were.

"You must have learned it somewhere," she said. "You're always so vague."

"On the Cape," he said. "We spent a month each summer on the Cape." But he had known it before that. "I saw somebody do it and just tried it out."

"So easy," she said. She closed her eyes and pushed with one hand and pulled with the other. She smiled.

He rowed gently up the stream. Reach after reach opened before him, glassy, dark, and still. Once a large dark bird flapped away heavily and out of sight around a bend before he could call her attention to it. But other than that the banks were deserted. Once the stream narrowed and seemed about to become too small to row in. He caught his oars in bushes and nudged the bank. He stood up and poled a bit, and then the stream opened out again.

But where was he there for a moment with the stream narrowing and the water failing, the low flat banks growing higher and higher as in a dream? Then the trees and bushes fell away, and he saw the winding muddy channels and the spongy peat banks of a tidal marsh.

Of course. The time he was caught by the tide far up into the marsh and had been left with no water at all. He didn't dare leave the boat—and it was no little aluminum thing in those days either. He didn't dare be late for supper. He couldn't stay to wait for the tide and he couldn't go. His mother would scalp him either way. Whatever he did was going to be stupid. So he started to drag the boat over the mud and over the slick marsh grass, taking sometimes the path of least resistance, sometimes the shortest distance between two points.

He strained. He sweated. He reveled in oaths. He was portaging around Presque Isle—the Golden Boys (no oaths—well, maybe "By gar!"). He was dragging his boats to the attack of Quebec—Kenneth Roberts, oaths aplenty. He was dragging his sledge toward the pole—he dreamed of Peary, Amundsen, Scott—Scott above all. Clouds of frozen oaths hung about his head.

At last he had found water again. First enough to slide the boat in. Then enough to float it. Then enough to let him get in and pole. Finally enough to row the boat the rest of the way to the sea. He lowered himself over the stern and washed off the mud: plastered with mud from head to foot against mosquitoes, although actually the new mosquito ditches had almost eliminated them.

"What are you smiling about?" Judith said.

"I was just thinking about the greatest day of my life," he said.

"Tell," she said.

And he told. He told right down to the frozen oaths and the missing mosquitoes. He told about pain and fear. He told about triumph. "I did it," he said, marveling. "I really did it."

"Why is it," she said, "that you always talk about yourself? Why don't you ever want to talk about me? What I did. What I thought. Who I knew. What it was like. I don't know how much more of this I can stand."

He felt somehow that none of this was fair. That wasn't at all how it happened.

"You could have been interested in Canada. You could have asked about my Everglades."

"But—" he said. He had tried. There wasn't much he could do about Canada. All he had seen there was trees and lakes and Nanook freezing to death on the shore of Hudson Bay. But he had offered what he had on the Everglades, and she had not offered in return. She had just flashed once and disappeared. It was like those old coast artillery guns that rose on springs out of the ground and kicked back down with their own recoil. Flash. Bang. Gone.

"What was Canada like?" he said.

"Go to hell," she said.

He didn't know what to say now, but thought that maybe anything was better than nothing. "Out on the lake," he said, "I was thinking of the time I had all the kids in a boat on a lake in Massachusetts." She was probing the bush with her glasses, but he knew she was listening, preparing to store it up. He spoke directly into her ear.

"It was very windy. I had my heart set on rowing around an island at the other end of the lake. When I got behind the island and my wife couldn't see us anymore from the shore, she thought we had all drowned. She thought I had done it to spite her. That's the kind of monster she thought I was."

"She was wrong," Judith said implacably.

He wanted to ask her what kind of monster she thought he was, but he didn't have to. His wife's words were good enough: "Monster of selfishness." It was pretty depressing to find himself right back there again.

He was rowing softly on and beginning to wonder where he would find the point for turning back. It wasn't as if there were an island to row around. The swamp seemed ready to go on forever, even without eagles—especially without eagles.

"Were you ever in a boat with your wife?" Judith said.

"I remember once," he said. "We were fishing."

"How was it?" she said.

"All right, I guess," he said. Somehow the memory wouldn't come. "We hadn't been married very long."

"You just can't admit it was ever any good, can you?" she said.

"I don't know that it was," he said.

"You didn't want to drown her then?"

"I don't know that I ever wanted to drown her. But I will admit that I thought of her being drowned, smashed in cars and trains, murdered in alleys and theaters. She never went anywhere that I didn't think, Maybe this is the time."

"I've been there," Judith said.

"Once she wrecked a car and walked away. She hit a split-rail fence and one of the rails came through the windshield and out the back window. She found it resting on her shoulder. I think we both felt it was a chance missed."

"Yes," Judith said. "Any end, just so it ends."

"Yes," he said.

"Do you want to drown me now?" she said. She was still scanning the bank.

He was rowing ever so gently. "Too shallow," he said.

"Just a tap with the oar," she said.

"There'd be a bump," he said. "Hard to explain."

"Not at all," she said.

"Look," he whispered. He had just worked around another bend and there, near at hand, were two does with fawns.

She looked. The boat drifted. The oars dripped. In their own good time the deer turned and picked their way back into the brush. Judith said, "Ah." It was as if she had been holding her breath all the while. The boat drifted aground.

"Pass me the oar," she said. "I'll pole us off." She stood up, beautifully balanced in the boat, and he passed her the oar. She maneuvered it over his head. Drops of water fell on him. She poled them off and turned to pass back the oar. Drops fell on him again. He sat meekly waiting. She towered over him. The oar swung slowly like a baseball bat toward him and then fell away toward the oarlock. He fitted it in. She sat down, composed herself, balanced the boat, and lifted her glasses from where they swung below her breasts. What did she know as the dotted drops of water fell on his head?

In the next reach of the stream they came to a beaver dam. It was old and partly demolished. Someone must have dragged a canoe through there. Perhaps he could get the boat through. On the other hand, this would be a natural limit. He looked beyond the dam and saw no end to the swamp. The stream went on to the next bend unchanged. If they had brought a lunch, sleeping bags, it would be different. Then they could go all the way, or at least to the end of the stream. After that they could walk.

"Shall we try it?" he said.

"We'd hurt the dam," she said.

"It's an old dam," he said.

"Are you sure?" she said.

"No," he said.

"Then let's go back," she said. "We'll be late enough for supper as it is."

"We're a long way up the creek, that's for sure," he said.

So they started home.

At almost the first bend they picked up the large dark bird. It flew ahead of them from bend to bend, rising heavily from the water's edge or dropping out of a tree, following the stream farther on and out of sight.

"It's not the eagle, I suppose," he said.

"No," she said, "nothing like it." She was still studying a clump of trees where the bird had disappeared. "I haven't been able to get a good look at it, but it's no eagle."

"Not big enough?" he said hopefully. He wanted an eagle to cover the sky with its wings, although of course he had seen eagles in the zoo.

"Built all wrong," she said.

"Shall I try to set you ashore if we can get close this time?" he said.

"Too much trouble," she said. But as he watched her glasses swing slowly as the boat got nearer and the angle changed, he resolved he'd try it. Damned if I do and damned if I don't, he said to himself.

"What did happen in that boat?" she said.

"What boat?" he said.

"When you were fishing."

"With my father?" he said, although he was pretty sure that was wrong. She didn't care all that much about his father.

"With her," she said. She glared at him over her binoculars.

And he knew she didn't mean his mother, although he had a quick picture of his mother seasick in the little boat tied up to a buoy while they were fishing for scup. An odd picture of his mother vulnerable.

"Oh," he said, "that boat. Nothing much. Nothing I remember. No American tragedy certainly."

"I wouldn't be so sure of that," she said. "I saw your face when the oar was over your head. It looked like a road show of *An American Tragedy* that ran for twenty-five years."

"Nothing happened," he said.

"That's what you always say," she said. "But now I know you're not telling it like it was. You did something or she did something. You thought of doing something or you caught her thinking it. There is something."

"Not that I know of," he said. He really didn't know of anything. The whole episode was very vague in his mind. In fact, he remembered it only as a snapshot of his wife sitting in the boat wearing his old clothes, her eyes veiled against the sun.

The stern of the boat bumped the bank, and Judith immediately stood up and stepped out while he clutched a bush to hold the boat steady. She quickly, cautiously made her way into the thicket. She was gone a long time.

It was only then that he was aware of an actual current in the stream. The boat kept drifting away from the bank, and he had to maneuver it back into position and hold the bush until he absentmindedly let it go again. Once he found himself well down the stream and knew it would be no Ameri-

can tragedy if he just drifted on and left her to find her way
out of the woods and back to the lodge. There would always
be ways for her to get back to the city. It wouldn't even be a
personal tragedy. But of course he worked the boat back
into place once more, and as if this were her cue, she
stepped out of the thicket.

"You should have come," she said. "I never saw anything
like it. She was just walking up the tree." She stepped into
the boat and settled herself.

She was so immersed in her marvel that she didn't notice
his cautious hesitation. "What do you mean?" he said.

"There was this tree," she said. "Blown over but not
down. Sort of slanting. And the bird was hopping up from
branch to branch like stairs. I can't explain it."

"What bird was it?" he said safely.

"A green heron," she said.

"Of course," he said.

"Of course," she said. "The most probable bird for a
place like this."

"A shit poke," he said. That was the boys' name for it.
There were shit pokes (but never called that) when he was
in boats with his father. Sea gulls on the buoy that time with
his mother. And pelicans that other time when nothing
happened.

"I wish you had come," she said.

"I should have," he said. "I was afraid for the boat."

When they finally went around the last bend and saw the
open lake, they found that the two boats of fishermen were
gone, but the ducks were still standing out in the middle of
the lake.

"Let's get a good look at the ducks anyway," he said, and
set his course by a large tree to the left of the inlet. Far down
the lake a man in a motorboat seemed headed toward them,
but he was probably going back to the lodge for supper.

Kiner was still a long way from the ducks when he felt his

oar strike something. He flushed with panic. *American Tragedy* came to him. He didn't even know if she could swim. Then it was obvious his oar had bumped the bottom, and the next instant the boat ran gently aground.

"So much for the ducks," he said. "The whole damn thing just missed being an island."

"How about mallards?" she said.

"Mallards it is," he said.

He pushed the boat off into deeper water and set a new course. The motorboat was now close to them. The man slowed the motor and stood up. He reached into the bottom of the boat and lifted a great fish, a muskie nearly as long as he was. Kiner and Judith waved. The man gently lowered the fish and stood up again, his arms extended over his head, fists clenched, like a soccer player running mad with triumph.

The Other Two

I ran into Peter Watts at the gym today. I had just stepped from the bath looking like a god—I know very well how I look. Enough women have told me. Enough homosexuals have made their passes. When I have a beard I look like George V or Nicholas, czar of all the Russias, and that's godlike enough for any man. I was on my way to my locker when I saw him. He was slumped on the bench, gray and old. He was so out of it that it seemed safe to stop and look at him.

Peter Watts lives with my ex-wife, so naturally I was curious. I was so curious, in fact, that finally I spoke to him, asked him if he was all right. Of course he was all right. Everybody slumps in front of his locker sometimes and listens to his heart and wonders if this is it at last or if health and eternal youth are worth such agony. Then quiet sets in, a drowsy blank that would be worth even greater pain.

He looked at me and knew me. I wasn't sure he would. It's been a long time, although we were familiar enough once. My ex-wife—Indiana her name is. I'm getting tired of the effort required to say ex-wife, so I'll call her Indiana. At one time I paid a therapist enough to teach me to say ex-wife: You have no wife, he said patiently until I lost patience and learned.

Indiana was Peter Watts's student once, when she first came to the university. That was before we were married—

childhood sweethearts and all that sort of thing. He hated me but never knew why. He was unhappily married himself. Of course, if he had really known about me and Indiana he wouldn't have been so jealous. I made her life miserable. I was a real son of a bitch.

She always worked and saw me through half the curricula in the university while I tried to find myself, as they say. I tried English. I even had a course with him because Indiana thought he was so great. He was OK. I was OK, too. He gave me an *A*. He had to. I saw to that. He hated it but I left him no choice. I also tried pottery before I finally fell among the computers where I discovered my true genius. In all modesty I can say that I am so good that I can work when I want and where I want for as long as I want, which is never very long. But there is always plenty of money. And plenty of women, of course. But there were always plenty of women. Not very surprising for a man who looks like a czar or a king-emperor—without my beard, the young Edward, Prince of Wales, is more my line.

I would have said I bear Indiana no ill will. She rather disgusts me, but that's quite another matter. If anything, she was always too good. Once in the middle of our marriage I even moved a woman into the house and sent Indiana off to sleep in some corner upstairs with the kid—John, that is. It's only natural, I suppose, that a woman named Indiana would name her kid John. I demanded breakfast in bed for me and the woman—I've forgotten her name—and Indiana brought it. Oh, I was a bastard. Indiana thought she was moving with the times. She thought that was the way people lived now. She was just a country girl, of course. What did she know? Indiana, indeed. Sometimes I wanted to kick her the way you want to kick a dog that doesn't have any self-respect. But ill will? No, never a trace of it.

I can imagine her saying now from the sublime height of her therapy that this is all guilt on my part. Guilt that I treated her like a dog. Guilt that I abandoned her. Guilt above all, compounding itself, because I want to see her really punished for some unnameable crime against me. I can't imagine what the crime is.

Nor do I bear Peter Watts any ill will. To be sure, he once refused to invite me to a party for some visiting hotshot writer who was being utterly wasted on those English Department types. Bellow perhaps. Or Barth. Or maybe Elkin, who really used to blow my mind in those days. But that seems scarcely enough to warrant the interest I take in him and my clear desire to learn that he and Indiana are making each other supremely miserable.

This Peter Watts was always an enigma, perhaps not to everyone but certainly to me. I never did know him very well, of course. He was somehow always at a distance, calmly following mysterious patterns of his own, and one of his most mysterious patterns was his long allegiance to that awful woman, his wife. But even more mysterious was his sudden desertion when such foolishness should have been long since over.

It was from my son—John—that I first learned Peter had moved into Indiana's house. I see John on weekends, and I listen to him, as I suppose, all divorced fathers listen to their children for hints as to what that woman is doing now, what kind of life she has made for herself, what she has done with Aunt Elsie's silver punch bowl—anything to illuminate that life now gone all dark. So I listen greedily to the details of Peter's lovely room, a book-lined study with a sofa bed moved in. At least they are keeping up appearances for John's sake. I rejoice in the inconvenience and in the hypocrisy, which I know must rankle in view of Indiana's new openness. She must hate it. Good. Good. And I ask John if one Big Mac is really enough. I get a lot of things for my hamburgers and shakes and fries—not allowed by

Indiana, who somewhere along the way has turned into a kind of health food freak.

This search for information has also led me to a technique that is absolutely direct. I lie in wait for Peter Watts. I plot his course. That was why I was at the gym. He swims every day. Indiana must love that—I was so unreliable. I didn't expect to get much out of him because he never liked me at all from the beginning when Indiana and I were his students, but we got to talking easily enough.

I thought at first he had forgotten who I was. Surely he wasn't going to be able to live with my wife—ex-wife—day by day and not learn that I contaminate the air about me and all I touch. Surely disgust would show in his face. But, no, he started right in as if he barely knew me and hadn't yet had time to hear, see, or speak evil of me. I won't say it made me uncomfortable, but I was certainly aware it was a novel situation. In fact it struck me as very civilized.

The divorce, on the other hand, was not at all what I would call civilized. It began with cold disgust on both sides and heated as the lawyers delicately peeled us down to our artichoke hearts of spite and venom, our purest humanity. There even had to be a separate court action concerning the tent pegs, which had somehow managed to get left in the trunk of her car when I removed the tent one dark night. Not that I have used the tent or the pegs since I got them, but the tent was somehow mine for reasons that are now obscure to me. A tent indeed. Me in a tent. Although there is no doubt that at one time we slept in a tent in the heart of the wilderness and listened to the usual night sounds, dogs, radios, and crying children. There was even a time when we slept in the tent with a crying child of our own. But I find it hard now to associate myself with a tent or remember why I ever wanted it or made an issue of the pegs. Or for that matter why she insisted on—and got—a copy of *The Wind in the Willows* that had been mine when I was a kid. *Edward Price, his book,* it said as big as I could write. *His book.* Jesus. How nine-year-old occasions do return to haunt us, as the poet does not say but might as well have.

Once he got to talking, Peter Watts was full of details and asides and allusions and soul-searching, almost as if he had forgotten all over again who I was. What an owlish and boring man. Serves Indiana right. I know I was never boring at least. I may have left her but why not? Traditionally the wife works and the husband gets his degree and then dumps her for someone younger, better educated, and, hopefully, richer. Someone whose daddy—But, no, I just left her and she went on working for her own degree and for John as if she couldn't imagine what else to do. There's something admirable about it in a disgusting sort of way, as if she had been a premature feminist or something.

This Peter Watts turned out to be so boring that it's a wonder I didn't strangle him then and there. I certainly understood more about his awful wife from dealing with him than I ever learned from her. Oh, yes, I looked her up as soon as I heard he had moved in with Indiana. Threw a few fucks into her, one of my standard ways of getting information. I often think I am like Mata Hari, fucking her way to all sorts of miscellaneous information.

I didn't learn much from Peter's wife. She is a good fuck, I'll say that, eager, inventive, and above all appreciative. Grateful even—as well she might be after all those dry years. She did have a tendency at the beginning to want to mark me, but I quickly cuffed her out of biting and scratching, and we got on very well in bed. Strictly in bed. But if she is a tartar, she is only what he has made her. Even a saint would be soured by such a boring man.

I had to listen to the description of his room all over again. I had to endure endless evenings by the fire while he read Trollope aloud to her and she knitted. Holy Jesus. I had to go with him to the river bank and imagine the place where he cut wood for the fire. There was a rhapsody on the light on the hills across the river. He had all the breathless wonder and solipsism of the true bore. It seems to be a gift.

Still, all this gives me great hope for him as an instrument of torture. But I must remember to be careful, because I long ago learned that when you start using people as instruments you are likely to get more than you bargain for. You forget that they have ideas of their own and that you are very probably some sort of instrument in their calculations. That one I moved into the house that time—what was her name?—certainly surprised me. All the while I was thinking about what a good fuck she was, she was thinking about what a useful husband I'd make. She wasn't smart enough to keep it hidden, so I kicked her out and moved Indiana back downstairs—she already knew what kind of a husband I made.

I can't help thinking just the same that he will do something awful to Indiana. Not even her sweetness and light will be able to stand up under the glacial flow of his dullness. Not even that lovely openness she has learned from her shrink. I can just see that tolerant smile setting, freezing solid, shattering. That will send her back to the shrink, and we'll see what she learns this time, for she'll come out with something, of course, some new piety to bring back to her family—bless Charles Manson and the overtones he added to that already lovely word *family*.

There she is with her family—her extended family. How she can make the honey drip from all the clichés of the day as she establishes eye contact so deep she seems to be looking out your asshole. Eye contact. Extended family. Expressive anger. Vitamin C. Wok cooking. Sho-to-kan karate. Black liberation. Women's liberation. Gay liberation. Prisoner liberation. No nukes. Organic foods. Personal trust

and integrity. Universal love. Save the seals—or whales—
or snail darters. Even with the best will in the world I don't
have enough expressive anger to continue the list.

I know that first therapist, by the way. We had a good
thing going there for a while, but she was too spacey for me.
She swung both ways and didn't know if she was coming or
going. When Indiana found out about us, she regretfully
terminated the professional relationship but still wanted to
remain friends. Of course you don't become friends with
your therapist, and above all you don't remain friends when
she fucks you over. Very unprofessional for the therapist
too, of course. But that's the way Indiana is. She holds onto
friendships. She will not let go. There are sacred bonds.
Mystic bonds. Bonds stronger than any fucking-over can
break. Except in my case naturally. Perhaps marriage is not
one of those bonds.

But apparently the connection between father and son is.
At least I find myself endlessly interested in John. Probably
a father can be forgiven an interest in his son, even such an
unconventional father as I. Every time you shoot your load
into a woman, you wonder how the kid would turn out—
and if you don't, she is sure to remind you. Of course I
don't have to conjecture at all. There John is, a golden boy
even in the eyes of his father, who would have been only too
glad to see every flaw of Indiana's returning to haunt her in
this form. But beyond that, I wanted to know what they
were making of him out there, what Indiana had done to
him in the years alone, what Peter was managing to achieve
as a role model.

Fortunately—or maybe not—Peter seems to enjoy the
role of instructor. This is, after all, his first chance at a boy
after devoting his life to his daughter, an unrewarding effort
to say the least, a ruined experiment to judge by what I
know of her. And it is right here that my interest is greatest:
will my son learn what I think I have learned about power

in the world? I don't believe I could teach him or anyone about these things. I don't know how I have learned them myself, but I do know them—or at least know how to use them. I should of all things like John to be adept here. I should like to see him trying his power on Indiana. She could not renounce him as she renounced me. She would have to endure it—yield or break.

No wonder I am fascinated by the idea of my son there in her house like a sleeper agent, like a trusted guard dog secretly primed with the latent command of MURDER, in short, a son. No wonder I want no part of him myself. Still, I listen. I watch. Even Indiana herself gives me crumbs of information as we pass him from hand to hand on weekends. I add it up. I improvise. I extrapolate. I bank it all, and I think I am not far from the truth. The truth may not be exactly what I would have it, but it is always pregnant. My options are always open. I don't even whisper BREAK HER. But that is constantly in my mind. It underlies everything I say. It shapes what I prepare for the distant future.

Curiously, although John clearly neither likes nor trusts me, he is more open with me than with Peter, whom he does like and does trust and whom he has elected his father. Not that I am jealous: let the family destruction fall on Peter's head when it comes. I'm all for that.

Naturally Indiana was not standing still while all this was going on. She was wheeling and dealing and moving and shaking. She was adding still another ring to the show at her big top out on the river road—after all, in Indiana's big Federal house, there are many mansions, and at that moment she and John and Peter were rattling around there by themselves.

I shouldn't have been surprised by anything, of course, because it's not for nothing that she is an expert consultant in small-group management—manipulation, as I prefer to call it. She has always been good at it, but her therapy has helped her identify it and market it. She can be as open as she likes, but I can still read her like a book in spite of all the crystalline disguises of her therapy.

It was at this moment in our conversation that Peter Watts surprised me. It certainly doesn't pay to assume that anyone hasn't a surprise in him, even the Peter Wattses of this world. I should have known better. "Do you see that man?" he said. He indicated a man blow-drying his hair at the other end of the alley of lockers.

I saw the man. I knew him, not his name but as much as I cared to know of him. He is the kind of man who bounces into the locker room after the most strenuous exercise—he runs on the indoor track and lifts weights—he bounces in patting his perfectly flat belly and strips and goes to the shower where he whistles deafeningly and off key. Somehow no one seems to be able to whistle anymore. When I was a kid there were great whistlers. Philip Bowles, the lawyer, used to walk to his office whistling opera, and Freddie Lewis whistled in two voices at once while he delivered groceries. Billy Forster, the town idiot, used to be asked to whistle *The Star-Spangled Banner* at ball games. But no more.

That was really all I knew about the guy. I couldn't help looking at him. He demanded it. But I didn't see much. He was packed into his skin like a splendid firm sausage, but I had no confidence in the seasoning—no doubt something bland made to be served for breakfast at restaurants along the Interstate. He had a painted-on smile, and I knew his handshake would paralyze my hand for the rest of the day and put an end to a pianist's career. It was a case of loathing at first sight.

"That man," Peter said, "is your wife's present lover."

"Ex-wife," I said automatically.

I also automatically checked his cock. It was entirely unremarkable, a mini-version of himself, something to spear on a toothpick and serve with drinks.

Then, only a very bad second, I looked at Peter Watts. My head was whirring like crazy, but nothing was yet showing up on the printout. "Oh, yes," Peter said. "No doubt about it." I didn't doubt for a minute. "He comes every Friday night and leaves after breakfast on Saturday." That figured. Indiana would scorn the bourgeois Saturday night fuck and would break new ground by moving it to Friday.

The printout managed to stammer half a line. "But I thought that you—" I blushed. I. Blushed.

He smiled his divine idiot smile.

I began to see that I had a marvelous new ingredient to throw into the old pressure cooker. I imagined him in his room, stoking his fire, handling his heavy irons, awake all night and listening like Tim the Hostler, who loved the Landlord's Daughter, Bess, the Landlord's Daughter, listening to her love passages with the Highwayman: "his eyes were a glitter of moonlight, his hair was like moldy hay." I love that moldy hay, but I expect great things of the glitter. Tim, of course, betrayed the lovers to the Redcoats. I don't know what we do in the absence of Redcoats, but I expect great things of Peter Watts.

Indiana, of course, assures Peter that this is all right and proper and natural: it's the way people live now in a world where it is quite impossible to find all you want in any one person. And Peter, of course, cries out against this—in his heart, only in his heart. He is an incurable romantic and believes in all the old incurable things like love and the world well lost for love and the world consumed by love. He has never experienced any of it and has never seen evidence that any of it exists, but he believes passionately in all of it. Nevertheless, he understands what he can have and he accepts that, although there are still nights when he cries himself to sleep—Friday nights among them. And this is most strange in a man who assures me that he has no feelings, is totally anesthetized.

Perhaps it is also strange that Indiana, who prides herself on her practicality, her grip on reality, should believe that she can take all these things she can't hope to find in any one person, can take them and the people embodying them and make them sit down about her in perfect harmony. Perhaps in her belief in the power of reason she is even more of a romantic than Peter himself. Be that as it may, she does believe it, and she even tries to act on it, going well beyond romanticism and becoming something like quixotic.

Of course Peter sees none of this. Any action of Indiana's is in his eyes like a natural law. It may be inscrutable. It may be paradoxical. It may involve him in difficulty and anguish. But it is right. Credo, he says to himself, credo, and he beats his beating breast with a bloodied stone. Whatever it is, it is only right—and only what he deserves.

This is all very promising. I like to think of Peter belaboring his fire in the middle of the night. I hear the cautious clang of the fire tools, his self-control made audible. I like to think he has inherited the poker I liberated one drunken night from a burned-out house. What a great heft it has. I'm glad it didn't occur to me to insist on that in the divorce settlement. It would smash a skull like an eggshell.

"Oh, no," Peter said, still with that smile. "I'm past it."

I wanted to ask him if it was Indiana who told him he was past it. As far as I could tell she never even got to it. She talked about it a lot afterward, but it must all have been very subterranean because no tremor of it ever reached her surface. Perhaps she got it all out of books. She always took great pride in having been a bookish child, and there were plenty of books lying around, mostly dating from the days when I believed I had more right to them than the library or the bookstore.

There was a lot more I wanted to ask him. Everything I had been imagining was all wrong, and nothing new was occurring to me on the spur of the moment. I did have a dim sense that I didn't like what they were doing to my kid out there in the way of role models. I sure as hell didn't want him to turn into one of those androgynous types so highly thought of by those Indiana types. Jesus. I didn't want no morphodite for a kid. My primordial fears—and grammar—were clearly being stirred up while I was momentarily off balance.

I wanted to ask all kinds of things, but before I could think of them, there was another surprise. That hulking kielbasa finished drying his hair and swaggered over to us, his cock waving in the breeze and his blower dangling from his hand like some kind of Flash Gordon ray gun.

"Hello, Peter," he said. "Hello, Ed. I'm Carter Kent." That was really a great name for a sausage. He ground up my hand, bone and all. I knew it would be paralyzed for the rest of the day, that my career as a pianist was finished. But there is a good deal of pleasure in the pain of being right.

"Well," Carter Kent said, "here we all are." His smile was idiotic without a trace of the divine. I saw the three of us there as if Indiana had planned it. I could even hear her assuring Peter that he and Carter Kent were both being very silly. Naturally she has friends for this and friends for that and sees no reason why these friends shouldn't get along with each other. What after all—oh, I can hear the noble rationality—what is the conflict between a fucking friend and a walking-on-the-levee friend, a Trollope-reading friend, a presence-in-the-house friend? Very silly indeed. And further, there is no conflict between either of these and an ex-husband friend.

"Here we all are," I said. Peter started and looked guilty. Two women spoke in the locker room over our heads. Their words were indistinct but their voices were clear and suggestive. Their bare feet padded to the showers. I studied the ceiling, tracked their progress as I often do. The other two glanced up. The showers roared. What a turn-on. I swear Carter Kent's unremarkable cock gave a very remarkable twitch.

"I've been looking for you," Carter Kent said, his head still turned in the direction of the upstairs showers. I was astonished to say the least, but it quickly turned out that it was Peter he was looking for. "I really meant what I said. I'm checking out. I just want you to know that."

"I'm sorry to hear it," Peter said. He was sure as hell sorry about something, but I wasn't sure that was it. His face was going gray, and he was slumping into himself as if he had at last gone too far in his exercises.

"No more of that bullshit," Carter Kent said. "It's getting too dikey around there for me."

"We usually call it the levee," Peter said.

"Fucking matriarchy," Carter Kent said. Peter made deprecating gestures like a third-base coach, hands, head, shoulders signaling some cryptic anguish. "You were right," Carter Kent said, looking at me.

"Just lucky, I guess," I said.

He looked at me in disgust and dismissed me. Very unwisely, I could have let him know, but I could bide my time. This was too interesting to spoil.

"That fucking May," Carter Kent said. Yes, I said to myself, May would be the wonderful one with the truck and the black belt in karate John was so impressed by. She was going to let him take down the motor next time she worked on it. A real marvel. She would also be the one from the Coordinating Committee on Women's Studies.

"You're welcome to my share of her," Carter Kent said.

"May?" Peter said. "No, thank you." He perked up for a moment once he was able to get into a word game.

"Indiana," Carter Kent said. "You can have my Fridays and anything else you can get—not much."

Peter sagged again. He looked as if he had been caught casting lots for Indiana's garments.

"Welcome to the club," I said to Carter Kent. I can't say I much cared for belonging to a club with a hot dog, but I did enjoy the thought of Indiana abandoned again. And I will say for the hot dog that he didn't seem to like the idea any more than I did.

"If you can stand it, of course," Carter Kent said. Peter didn't show anything. "How can you stand it? No politicians except women. No truck drivers except women. No writers except women—your fucking Trollope just happened to have a lucky name. How *do* you stand it?"

"My consciousness has been raised," Peter said as if it had been raised right out of his skull. "But she promised," he said to me—to *me*. He looked at me. I nodded. He only wanted comfort. And what had she promised? She had promised some simple-ass thing, a walk on the levee on a fine spring day. But someone had needed her. Someone always needed her more than he did. And could his needs always be put off? Could he always be expected to understand? Could he always find it in his heart to be fair? He was perfectly aware he wasn't being fair, but he didn't want to be fair. He was hurting and he wanted to hurt back, and his hurt was only increased by the knowledge that she would simply shrug and say all that had nothing to do with her, that he was just being difficult. Of course *That's your problem* would be the cliché for that particular situation.

By now he was no longer talking to me but was deep down into himself. Although this was an Indiana very different from the one whose heart bled all over me, I can't say I liked her any better. I nodded again. He insisted that even in the midst of his screaming and shouting and chewing the rug—strictly in the privacy of his room, of course—he wanted to show her that he understood and was dismally afraid that what he showed was that he didn't understand at all. He didn't even know what he was supposed to understand. It was all verbs without subjects and pronouns without antecedents.

"You better chuck her before she chucks you," Carter Kent said.

"Oh, no," Peter said. Horror made him sit up straight and stare at Carter Kent and at me. "I couldn't do that."

"It's in the wind," Carter Kent said. "You'll go. The kid will go. You'll see."

"John—" Peter whispered.

"He'll go to his father," Carter Kent said. "They've got it all figured. They'll call it poetic. They're big into poetic. The little rat goes to the big rat. The little snake goes to the big snake—ugh, ugly. The little snakes are venomous when they come out of the shell. They should be crushed at once. They just represent some man doing something nasty to a defenseless woman."

"To me?" I said. I was as nearly dumbfounded as possible. "What a vision."

"To you," Carter Kent said.

"But I'm a shit, a prick, and a bastard," I said.

"An acid freak," Carter Kent said.

"A pothead," I said.

"A wife beater," Carter Kent said. He looked at Peter.

"A swine," Peter said weakly. But he began to get into it as we went on developing the litany of my wrongdoing. In fact, we nearly got kicked out of the gym before we were done. Peter was shouting and screaming and pounding on his locker, and we had to keep him from hurting himself.

"It's all right, tiger," Carter Kent said. "She's not worth it."

"It's all I've got," Peter said. He slumped back into himself.

Carter Kent and I looked at each other over his head and sat on either side of him and put our arms over his shoulders and said nothing.

Revenge

When Peter Dillon got off the bus at his hotel near the Angel in Mexico City, he took two steps and felt for his billfold. It was gone. He smiled. He was content. But as he approached his hotel he became aware of a man running toward him, waving his arms and cursing violently—at least Dillon assumed he was cursing. He had lived long enough in cities to know that there are crazies everywhere, many of them given to waving their arms and cursing if not often to running. He moved to one side to allow the man to pass, but the man veered toward him. Dillon moved aside. The man veered.

Then Dillon was on the ground. He was contemplating shoes. Mexicans in the city do not wear sandals, he acutely observed. He also translated without difficulty the words *gringo* and *borracho*. He rolled an indignant eye and picked out a policeman wearing the familiar badge that showed he spoke English.

"I am indeed an American," he said, "but I am not drunk. I have been robbed and beaten in the middle of the Reforma under the very eye of the Angel." He rolled his eye further to take in the rest of the crowd and noted that the man who had beaten him had become an interested bystander with no one appearing to be the wiser. The man smiled. Dillon managed a smile of his own. "*Claro,*" he said, his third and perhaps his last Spanish word.

He saw the man's face darken. He saw his lips move as he

repeated "*Claro,*" his face full of dark confusion as he strug-
gled to grasp whatever further outrageous but obscure insult Dillon had intended by simply agreeing, *yes, clearly, to be
sure.*

"*Loco,*" the policeman explained to the crowd. It turned
out that Dillon had four Spanish words.

In the hospital Dillon had time to review his success—
there was no doubt it was a success. That man would have
beaten him again if the policeman had not been standing in
the way. As it was, he could only rage and glower as Dillon
was placed in an ambulance and carried away out of his
reach. Decidedly the whole affair had been a triumph for
Dillon. He rested well. He had had his revenge. It had been
a long time coming, but he had had it.

In the beginning, twenty years and more before, he had
had his pocket picked in the classic manner on the Route
100 bus, the very bus everyone is warned about, that and
Mariachi Square where he had wandered safely the night
before. He had assumed that if he could make his way
among those throngs of unemployed musicians he must be
invulnerable. Of course he was not invulnerable. He was
only a challenge.

He had just swung to the ground and the bus had only
just begun to roll away from him when he knew what had
happened. He ran after the bus and beat on it with his
hands, but it accelerated and left him hopelessly behind. It
was rage that he felt. Indignation. He had been invaded. It
wasn't the money—or at least it wasn't the money to any
serious extent. To be sure, he had lost more than he cared to
lose, but then he didn't care to lose anything. It wasn't as if
he had lost it at the fronton, although he never bet. It
wasn't as if he had spent it on foolish things—he never
shopped. It wasn't as if he had shot his wad on some un-
imaginable orgy—he was the most abstemious man he
knew. No, he had had nothing for it. He had not had the

excitement of a losing game, of tourist booty, not even of a hangover and regrets. On top of that, he had suffered indignities such as he had never known.

As he sat that night on his balcony overlooking the Reforma—and the Route 100 buses—he drank his usual two carefully measured bourbons mixed with purified water and cooled with certified ice. He preferred not to remember that he had once seen an iceman scooping spilled ice cubes off the ground and dumping them into a plastic bag of exactly the sort he had at other times seen delivered to the hotel. It was impossible to control everything.

It was impossible to go back to that moment just before he got off the bus when the man ahead of him, the man waiting in the back stairwell of the bus, had dropped a handful of coins about his feet. Careful reflection had enabled him to isolate this moment as the one when his hand should have gone automatically to his pocket. He knew there was no going back. He hadn't noticed even the decoy except as a pair of hands scrabbling about his feet. Still, he ached for revenge.

He fantasied the moment. He caught the hand of the pickpocket in a steely grip and brought him to his knees with a jujitsu twist—Dillon's fantasies, he was quick to admit, were somewhat antiquated and hadn't yet incorporated the more innovative arts of karate and kung fu. On the other hand, when he imagined shouting "Thief" on the crowded bus, the other passengers righteously turned on him and he found himself in a Mexican jail. Even his fantasies often betrayed him and offered nothing but dampening views. Still, in spite of this and in spite of the fact that there was only a nameless, faceless enemy, he contemplated revenge.

The revenge had to wait, however. The next day he retrieved his traveler's checks from the hotel safe and set out for home as scheduled. He traveled fast and without rest. It was his constant fear that he would arrive too late, that someone with all his identity would have arrived at his house and established himself securely. Not only that, but he was sure that this person, this small Mexican with a small mustache, would be better liked by his wife, his children, his neighbors, and his employer and that he himself would be turned away, nameless, and perhaps even deported to Mexico.

The fact that none of this turned out to be true reassured him—but only a little. The person could still appear, flash his impeccable credentials, and turn him out. "I always thought so," his wife would say. His employer would rub his hands in relief and graciously not bring in the police, frowning the while as if doubting his own wisdom and questioning the folly of his own good nature.

Meanwhile, Dillon continued to contemplate revenge. He perfected a hundred plans of highly romantic and impractical natures. He saw himself—almost in mask and cape—becoming the scourge of Route 100 pickpockets, destroying the ring, exposing the complicity of the drivers, bringing to light the corruption of the police. Hi ho, 100, away.

But gradually he settled on a scheme less romantic but still satisfying and apparently without danger to himself. He would ride the buses with a dummy billfold in his pocket and invite the pickpockets to do their worst. In the early versions of this scheme, the billfold was attached to his belt by a stout chain. He would run the chain through a hole in his pocket and, thoroughly concealed, up to his belt. For a while he even added an alarm to the chain and tried to work out a handcuff that would automatically clamp onto the thief's wrist. Then the scheme reversed itself, and he eliminated handcuff, alarm, and chain and introduced instead a simple slip of paper bearing a simple message.

The message, however, was not easy to decide on. It had, if not to express his own rage, to generate a comparable rage in the thief, any thief. "April Fool" would not do. And his own rage was too vast for any catch phrase or slogan. He was very much at a loss until his Spanish phrase book came to his rescue. He was looking under Insults, Invective, and Imprecations when he chanced upon "*Chinga tu madre,*" which the book chastely translated as "Rape your mother" and assured him was the one unforgivable insult. He was somewhat disappointed. He had expected Spanish to be more fertile of invention than that, but he was willing to accept the editor's authority and many editions. What had happened to him was unforgivable and he wanted only to reply in kind.

The next time he was sent to Mexico he carried his carefully prepared billfold, a cheap one but new. After his appointments he rode the bus between his hotel and the anthropological museum until he was exhausted. Disappointed, he returned to his room, poured the first of his drinks, and sat down to inspect his bait for any flaws. To his astonishment the paper on which he had carefully printed his message to the world had been reversed, and he now read: "So's your old man."

He was depressed. He was up against a more formidable adversary than he had believed. Further, his faith in his message was shaken. "So's your old man" was doubtless out of an English phrase book, and as a result the credibility of all phrase books came into question in spite of any assumed authority and any number of editions. However, there was no one he could ask about his little phrase. It wasn't exactly the sort of thing he liked to mention to the Mexican clients of his firm, nor did he care to try it on, say, a cabdriver or shoe-shine man. He felt no doubt that he could say it right, but he had no confidence that he could explain his interest before he had a knife run into him, if indeed it should turn out to be more potent than "So's your old man." That night he lost track of things and actually drank three drinks.

The next day, the last of his stay, he struck pay dirt at

once. The first time he got off the bus at the Museo de Antropologia he had the sensation of having started a chain reaction. Behind him was a man with his hand stuck to the dummy billfold, and behind that man was another man in the very act of slapping a handcuff onto the first man's other wrist. It was so like Dillon's fantasy that he could only stare.

The policeman snatched the billfold and waved it about. "Evidence," he said in perfect English. "How much money?"

"No money," Dillon said in no less perfect English—he was on his mettle.

"No money?" the policeman said. He clearly felt there was a failure of communication, because he looked into the billfold. Immediately his face darkened. He whirled the pickpocket about like a lasso, and Dillon found himself chained fast by the other handcuff. Unfortunately in his haste and anger the policeman had chained them right hand to right hand so that they looked as if they were in the act of bungling a simple handshake, and when they moved to the patrol wagon it was Dillon who had to walk backwards.

The visit to the police station was not edifying. First, Dillon was charged with insulting a police officer in the performance of his duty. "Your mother wears army boots," the offended policeman said when the charge was recorded. At least his phrase book seemed to be some forty years closer to being in date. The only comfort Dillon could find was the assurance that his insult did, in fact, seem to be a bona fide insult of the first water.

However, the real trouble began when he was searched and his actual billfold came to light in his special secret inner pocket. The policemen passed it from hand to hand and checked his ID's. They nodded wisely and made very Mexican sounds which Dillon tentatively interpreted as "Aha!"

The charges now became theft and misuse of credit cards. There was a long account to settle. He had evidently led the Mexican police a merry chase. It was their turn now and they were going to make the most of it. "I'm being accused," he told the company lawyer when he finally was allowed a telephone call, "of stealing and misusing my own credit cards." But he was still not in the clear. He remained in jail for three days, and only the direct intervention of the Embassy brought about his release.

"You'll have to be more careful," the Embassy told him.

"This puts us in a very bad light," the company said.

"It was in all the papers," his wife said.

He thought he would lose his job or at the very least never be sent to Mexico again, but as it turned out, the Mexican clients took to asking specifically for that so-amusing Senor Dillon, and he became, in spite of himself, almost indispensable. His job was secure but his revenge eluded him as much as ever.

His next two visits to Mexico were fruitless. He rode the buses religiously, but the plainclothesmen glowered at him, known pickpockets gave him the Mexican finger, and bus drivers threw his change on the floor. Once, indeed, he thought he had scored, but the bus, which had started, stopped abruptly. The back door opened, and a plainclothes policeman hurled his billfold at his head. He was discouraged and began to see himself as a kind of Flying Dutchman self-condemned to ride the 100 line forever or an Ancient Mariner forever deprived of a Wedding Guest to ease his pain.

Then, strangely, his fame seemed to have faded. New generations of police and pickpockets knew him not. New generations of bus drivers accepted his exact change without a sneer. He felt almost abandoned, almost as if he were starting all over again, older, tireder, and with little hope of ever achieving a goal he had almost forgotten.

The message in his billfold was faded now, the paper

dirty and crumbling at the edges. He was afraid that "*Chinga tu madre*" would no longer pass current, but he hadn't the interest to check it in any of the newer phrase books. He was simply riding the buses now because that was what he did when he came to Mexico. Even he knew he had become a harmless eccentric, a man with one very odd spot in his makeup.

It happened, then, when he was no longer paying attention, that he got back to his hotel one night to find his dummy billfold missing. He felt at first that he had been deprived of something, something important, that something that really mattered had been wrenched out of the fabric of his life. Then as the sweat-stained billfold, the tattered message came back to him, he remembered his revenge.

He tried to feel elation but he felt nothing. He tried to understand that he had completed a lifelong quest, but nothing at all seemed to have ended. He went back to the beginning, to that day his pocket had been picked, and there he found anger. He beat once more on the back of the bus with his fists. He shouted, "Thief." His heart raced. He broke into a sweat. One more tiny twist would break the thief's arm like a matchstick. He had been wrong all those years thinking it would be enough to know that the thief had taken the bait, was reading the message, was wanting to break his limbs one by one, to slice him with a dull knife, to roast him over a slow fire, and all without having any idea who he was or where to find him, he, Dillon, having been until that moment at best merely a professional problem involving a pocket and a billfold.

Deprived now of his revenge just when he thought he had achieved it, deprived even of his old familiar lure, Dillon could only go blindly back into the old pattern. Without hope now, he bought a new billfold. He wrote a new message without even caring if it was still in a language used by living men.

And then, once again, and the very next day, he was standing on the sidewalk looking after a bus. He watched it all the way to the next stop, feeling the vacancy in his hip pocket, the emptiness in his heart. He watched the people boil out of the bus and one man detach himself from the group and begin to run back along the route of the bus. The man was stumbling in his haste, churning his arms and legs as if in a mad attempt at a takeoff, a heavy water bird slow to rise from the surface, dabbling the pavement with his tiptoes. As he came close, Dillon could hear his shouts.

Dillon knew the cities were full of crazies, mostly harmless, so he effaced himself, but the man clearly had him in mind and only him. They maneuvered on the sidewalk as if actually they were trying to avoid each other with the best will in the world. And such was Dillon's well-practiced skill in avoiding that the man nearly did run past him, but just at the crucial moment he threw an object into Dillon's face— the new billfold, the ancient message. Stopped in the midst of his most skillful maneuver, Dillon was run down, trampled, bloodied, and pulped.

Ah, he said to himself. This was rage. This was what he himself had felt and what he had wanted all these years in return, rage so enormous that no violence could assuage it, no mountain of heaped indignities reduce an atom of its monstrous debt. His fall to earth was gentle. The pain of being moved to the ambulance was a recognition in every bone that his revenge was complete. His bones would mend, his blood restore itself. He had now only to contemplate a placid age, a contented death.

Wild Geese

In his dreams she was always going away from him— going down corridors, going down escalators, jumping off buses. Of course he knew what that was all about, but the dreams went on anyway. Not that he was surprised. Even awake he couldn't accept the fact that he wanted to leave her.

She was running down the long stairs at the Shepherd's Bush Station, at the bottom while he was still at the top. She gave up her ticket and turned right and went into the street. When he came out, she was nowhere to be seen. "What do we do at this point?" he said distinctly. "We take the 31 bus home," he replied. So he ran to the bus stop but didn't find her. It was all wrong, of course. When he went to Shepherd's Bush, he went alone to the Rangers' stadium. The 31 bus didn't go there at all. He would walk along Loftus Street laughing at the bearded satyr face on the keystone of each window and each door. He called the face Loftus after a friend in New York.

Sometimes he dreamed about geese, high wavering lines of them, their cries coming faintly down like the belling of enchanted hounds. Sometimes they were very low and loud, just above the treetops as he had seen them one night. He knew what that was all about, too.

"Geese," she said, "are monogamous. They mate for life." She always had the facts.

But mostly she was going away. They had got as far as New York together. They had gone through customs and had got on a bus to be taken into the city. It looked like Pier 40 to him. Holland-American Line. "Wait," she said and got off the bus. They all waited a long time. Then the bus drove off. She had the tickets and the hotel reservations. He didn't know where he was supposed to be going.

"What is it you really want to do?" his therapist said.

"I don't know," he said.

"I think you do," the therapist said.

"He wants to leave me," she said.

"Whose dream is this anyway?" he said. "It's mine. It's mine. It's mine." He tended to say things three times in his dreams as if to make them really his.

They were all his, of course. Every one of them. For richer or poorer, in sickness and in health. He was on his knees in the Garden of Gethsemane. He was looking at his disciples asleep around him. He looked them up and he looked them down and he said, "One of you will betray me." It wasn't so easy for him. He didn't know about Judas. He only knew that one of them was out to get him. And their names weren't names like Simon or Peter or Thomas or Matthew-Mark-Luke-and-John. Their names were Heart and Kidneys and Liver and Lungs. And one of them had already sold him out. Gallbladder was already dead, the lousy bastard, so he wasn't the one—he'd made his move and it wasn't good enough. He was down on his knees in that garden, sweating blood, knowing he'd had it.

Actually, that Gallbladder business had been a very close thing. It nearly did for him. And the rest of them were no help either. They were just standing around looking, except for the one who was banging away left and right, more likely to cave in his ribs than anyone else's. The others would have jumped him if they had dared. He saw it happen to the man in the next bed. They choked him and turned him blue. His breathing was awful. Unforgettable. He knew his own gang was taking it all down and filing it away. But they didn't quite dare yet, although they were sullen the next day when he tried to call them to order. When he was let up to go to the john for the first time, he said, "All right, you scum, where are you?" He sat there sweating and weak and sending out all the messages he could think of, but they took their time and let him know he was slipping.

"It is only what you must expect at your age," she said.

"And what is my age?" he said.

"At your age," she said, "you have a further life expectancy of 26.3 years."

"No more?" he said.

"No more," she said.

"I want it," he said.

"I shall see that you get it," she said.

He heard geese in the night. They were very loud and a long time passing. Geese still flew for his birthday. He counted on it, just as he had once counted on the Fourth of July to happen for his father's birthday. After his father died, the Fourth of July somehow never happened again but the geese went right on flying. Even after the great fair that went with the geese was moved to warmer weather, the geese went on, and the fair never happened again either. It was a remarkable thing: "All you have to do is look," the man said. "They're always there if only you'll look." And he looked. And the geese were there, silent in the infinite moonlight, clear and slow above the pine trees of the picnic grove. And all the people cried out. And the aerialist swung unnoticed to a stop. And the fireworks fizzled in the grass of the infield.

"Now, this fall," she said, "perhaps I can get you a goose for your birthday. My father always got a goose in the fall. I can remember to this day the sound the shot made as people spit them out on the good china plates. Ping. Ping.

'More trouble than it's worth,' my mother said. 'Not at all,' my father said. And it wouldn't be, not if you'd like it."

"No, no," he said. But she did it anyway, and he ate it. It's only poultry, he said. It's only poultry. It's only poultry.

"I've got to go to the ladies'," she said and went off toward the back of the restaurant. He had a drink and then another. He tried to catch the waitress to go look for her, but they were all eating at a big table in the corner or running around aimlessly. One was running among the tables in graceful arcs like a dancer, trailing long brilliant draperies. She became smaller and smaller as she ran, not quite human, almost a butterfly in all those colors. There was no help for it. The waitresses were useless. She was surely gone. He began to gather up her usual things. There was a knitting bag crammed with books and papers and a shopping bag also crammed. There seemed to be much more, but investigation showed that the other two bags were empty, although they were standing up as if full. He picked it all up and started for the door. Halfway there he remembered he had forgotten her coat. "Oh, shit," he said, because he had a cramp in his right instep, the way you are aware that if you go on stretching your legs like that you'll bring on a cramp but it's already too late and you say, Oh, shit. There was no coat when he got to the table, but there was a note. It wasn't the same table anyway. It was the table in their flat. The note said she had called all the guests and canceled the dinner.

"You might have known," she said, "that I couldn't have all those people in at once. Any *man* would have known it." She had a way of saying *man* as if it were the name of a god she had never seen.

"But you forgot the Gulbrakians," he said, and was instantly glad she wasn't there to hear him.

"You bastard," she said. It wasn't that easy to get off.

He tried to call her on the phone. He stood looking across

the courtyard to the other wing of the building, but he couldn't pick out her window. "Hello," she said, very faint. It was a bad connection.

"Hello," he said.

"I can't hear you," she said, fading almost to nothing.

"Did you," he said, "call the Gulbrakians?"

There was a faint hum in the rhythm of speech but nothing more. He hung up and dialed again but her line was busy. He ran down the stairs. There were lots of stairs. Flight after flight of them around the wide square well. They met in the courtyard.

"Did you remember—" he said.

"Will you take me to lunch?" she said.

"Never mind that," he said. "Did you—"

"Will you take me to lunch?" she said. There was an enormous and obscene smile on her face.

"Later," he said. "Later. Did—"

"I'm going to keep your drawer straight," she said. He saw his underwear and his socks standing at attention in his drawer.

"I'm sure I thank you very much," he said.

"I think—" she said.

"I don't give a shit what you think," he screamed. He knew exactly how offended she would be by that kind of language, and he resented the fact that she could say anything she wanted. "Did—"

"Fuck off," she said. "You bastard," she said. Circumstances often forced her to express herself vividly. She went back up her stairs on the other side of the courtyard.

He went in and lay on the bed in the maid's room. His knapsack was hanging from a post at the foot of the maid's bed. Through the half-open door he could see the Gulbrakians come down the stairs. They were a very tiny, very European old couple, moving slowly and with all the lack of grace of their assured culture. "I wonder what has become of him?" Mrs. Gulbrakian said. Mr. Gulbrakian shrugged. "Americans," he said. They went up the other stairs. The maid was standing at the sink rinsing her dentures. She was talking a steady mush of what he took to be Polish. She was a large, strong old woman with iron-gray hair. "Back to that," he said. "Back to improbable women. The ugly. The dirty. The ancient. Baby girls. Harelips. At least she looks clean." The maid turned from the sink and came toward him.

"After all," she said, "it may not even be spaghetti by the time it gets to the help. It's been through the machine so many times it may be popcorn."

The dinner was going on anyway. The room was full of all the people invited, including the Gulbrakians. The children were there, smaller than for a long time, neatly dressed but with their sexes all anyhow. The room was very large. The floor was bare and unpolished, unpainted even, and darkened only by use. His bed was at one end of the room, unmade, and a kitchen was at the other. He was trying to work his way toward the bed to throw the covers unobtrusively over it.

"It was good of you to invite me," she said.

He glanced across the courtyard to try to pick out her window to see if she was at home. "That's all right," he said. He was standing between her and the bed, trying to hide it from her. He had a thick stack of IBM cards in his hands, and he ruffled them constantly. One fell at their feet. She picked it up and glanced at it before she handed it back. He knew it said *shame*.

"Another woman," she said. "So that's it." He let her think so. He was glad to. Somehow that was more manageable as an explanation.

"I pity her," she said. "She'll learn what it is to long for a man."

"Ah, well," he said.

"I've got to go to the ladies'," she said. And she went.

"It's time to eat," a woman said. So there was another woman. He wished he could see her. Perhaps these children with their sexes all wrong—yes, of course. The table was ready in the middle of the room. He found himself facing a window that opened onto an air shaft. Just across the air shaft was the bathroom window. He could see her shadow moving on the frosted glass.

"Let's begin eating," the woman said. They all began, but they ate very slowly. Even so, they finished and she hadn't come back. He mopped his plate with bread, all the while watching the shadow on the window and quite forgetting to sneak a good look at the woman at his table.

"The toilet won't work," a child said. It was obviously some other toilet.

The woman leaned out the window into the air shaft and shouted, "Flush it again. You're holding up the plumbing." There was some mysterious infirmity in the plumbing that let the water in the house run only when the toilet was flushed. He felt a warm glow of pleasure at this public display of particular and intimate knowledge. That was when she came back. She came into the room and walked in a large arc around the foot of the bed. When she was almost up to the bed, she put a small pistol to the base of her skull. "She'll never do it," he said. It was clearly all a bluff. The sound was sharp and small like a breaking twig. She continued around the bed and picked up the end of the sheet and said, "This is the percale sheet your mother gave us for a wedding present." She seemed genuinely hurt. Then she gave the sheet a shake to straighten it. Wrinkles flew. She lay down. He ran to the phone and dialed the operator and asked for an ambulance. "Yellow Cross has a broken tie-rod," the operator said, "so you'd better not call them. Try Speedy." There was almost no blood.

"So," she said, "you have left me."

He picked up his knapsack. He carried it everywhere instead of a briefcase. It contained, as it always did, socks and underwear and a clean shirt, traveler's checks and a flask of fine brandy. And a little book he had always wanted to read, a very slim volume. Or perhaps he was going to keep a journal in it.

Yes," he said. "I believe I have."

Reflections in the Ice

Everyone knew about my father's two wives. Some said he married my mother and then the other one. Some said he married the other one first and then my mother. One day, standing beside a hole in the ice where he was seining for shiners, Robert Martin described to me in great detail a wedding with two brides and my father in the middle. But Robert Martin smelled of vanilla extract that day like all other days and was probably confused in his attempt to express his admiration for my father, whose personal atmosphere was Scotch whiskey and who knew how to take Robert's shiners and catch even bigger pickerel than Robert himself. I had, after all, a sort of right to be out on the ice with Robert.

This about my father's two wives may sound very much like bigamy, but, unless I am mistaken, someone has to file a complaint for a charge to be brought, and who would complain of my father? Who could complain of him? He was a successful businessman and politician. His households were models of propriety. He drank good whiskey. He caught big fish. He went to mass at eight o'clock on Sunday morning and to Unitarian services at eleven.

When my mother and I walked out with him of an evening, the other one, if we met her, would bow to the eminently respectable hardware merchant and he would lift his hat to her. When my mother did her shopping in the morning, she bowed if she met the right respectable member of the school board out for a walk with the other one. He was a goodly, godly, respectable man.

And my mother was a respectable woman. She was straight and tall, and her ways were immaculate. She kept her house and her garden and her poultry and me in immaculate order. She had been a schoolteacher, and she kept his books for him and looked after his business correspondence. She was everything a wife and mother should be— and yet I had a sense of being shortchanged each time she offered that cool cheek just barely scented with the good soap she used, her soap.

Fortunately for my health of mind there was the other one. She was not at all like my mother. A glance was enough to show that she didn't come from our town, for she was dark and plump. We always believed she had been a shopgirl in the city, although Robert Martin once told me, for whatever it was worth, that she had been on the stage. However that may be, it is her kisses I remember. Her lips were very full and soft. I am tempted, in spite of knowing better, to say that I have never felt anything softer—I do say it—I have said it before now.

Why she should have been kissing me, I can't imagine. It seems highly unlikely that my mother would have selected her as baby-sitter—there are limits even to civilized behavior. But I was with her sometimes. I am sure of that. Sometimes when neither my mother nor father was there. As if, perhaps, my father had gone off on a trip and taken my mother with him. And there were other times, in the night, when she would come into my room. I think now she might have been at a party at our house. Very unlikely, of course. Perhaps I dreamed it. But the kisses are very real.

In addition to supplying my father with shiners, Robert Martin also helped out in the store whenever he happened to need cash or the weather was too bad for fishing. It would be a mistake, however, to conclude that my father was his patron. If any patronizing was done in that two-man democracy, Robert did it. He worked only when he wanted and as long as he wanted. He came and went as he liked, and my father, a doubly responsible man, stayed in the store summer and winter, rain and shine. On fine days when Robert happened to be working in response to some need of his own—usually vanilla extract—my father would often invent a delivery at the lake and would send him off and then settle himself down to the routine of the store and a quiet afternoon of vicarious truancy.

On these occasions Robert was always back by closing time—he was paid by the day—with a tale which usually involved a flat tire and his shiftless brother, who just happened to be passing with a fine mess of fish and who sent along something nice and fresh for my father's supper. Robert was invaluable to a man as burdened as my father. I know for a fact that one particularly lovely spring—it was the last of my father's life—Robert made a trip on the store's business to a supplier near Moosehead Lake in Maine. He was gone nearly a month—checking specifications, I think it was.

As far as I know, Robert and my father never discussed Moosehead Lake. In fact, it seems to me, now that I put my mind to it, that they discussed very little at any time, although each was known and esteemed in his own circle as a talker and storyteller. Be that as it may, on a foul day not long after Robert's return from Maine my father broke the silence in the store by saying suddenly, "Robert, would you mind spreading the Boston *Post* on the floor? I want to lie down."

Some people say Robert was so simpleminded that he always did whatever he was told without stopping to ask questions. My private opinion was that he was far more sensible than most adults, but perhaps a child's values are sometimes unrealistic. In any case, Robert spread the *Post* on the floor beside my father's desk as if he did it every afternoon of his life. My father stepped to the edge of the paper, oriented himself, and lay down. He straightened his coat, pulled down his vest, adjusted his watch chain, folded his hands on his breast, crossed his ankles, and closed his eyes. He was somewhat in the way in the cramped quarters behind the counter, but Robert respected his rights—it was a true democracy—and stepped over and around him all afternoon. Only when it was time to close the store did Robert speak to him to ask for the key. By then he had already been dead for some hours.

I don't know how much anguish there was over the problem of burying my father. Clearly it is one thing for a man to go to mass at eight and to Unitarian services at eleven and quite another thing for him to be buried twice. Successive funeral services, perhaps. Simultaneous graves, no. However, my father, prudent as always, had foreseen the difficulty and provided for it.

In those days the two churches were on the common, at opposite ends. The Catholic cemetery and the Protestant cemetery both extended northward from the common with a large field the width of the common between them. What my father had done was buy up this field—John Marsh's pasture—and will half of it to the Catholic church and half of it to the Unitarian church, reserving for himself only one plot on each side of the dividing line and stipulating that he be buried exactly on the line with a wife on either side of him. My mother's grave has been filled for a good many years now. The other is still waiting, and perhaps I'll never see it filled, but I am convinced that wherever she has been all these years and whoever she really is she'll come back in the end. But I'm getting ahead of my story.

After my father's death, our manner of life changed completely. It was no longer necessary for my mother and the other one to nod in the street. The bond between them was broken. They might, as widows, be friends, but they need not be even acquaintances. Now that I think back, I can't remember ever seeing the other one after we left the cemetery. She simply disappeared from my sight, from my consciousness.

My mother, on the other hand, grew and multiplied. She went directly from the cemetery to the store and opened for business. She took off her hat as if she were at home and sat down at the desk with the ledgers. She soon saw, however, that running the store by herself was a hopeless task. She needed help. Night after night she sat over her sewing or her ledgers and convinced me she needed help. I tried volunteering the first few times but discovered, greatly to my relief, that that wasn't what she meant at all. I was big and strong for my age, but I was still, after all, a boy. Then she stopped talking about it, and I assumed all was well.

Imagine my horror when I stopped in at the store for something—as a matter of fact it was fishhooks—and saw Robert Martin wearing a suit and even a tie as he worked behind the counter. He was cleanly shaved and very pale. He brightened for a bit as we discussed fishhooks, and he approved my choice of hook for the pond I intended to fish that day, but he was a very sick-looking man as he turned to rummage through a lot of boxes for a special hinge Mat Warren wanted for some cabinet work he was doing in the old Crawford place. I told him I'd bring him something nice and fresh for his supper, but he didn't seem to hear me, so I went about my business, although the day was appreciably darkened by the knowledge that I couldn't hope to find Robert Martin around the next bend of the river or watch him asleep in a drifting boat out in the middle of some pond. To be quite frank, he was at that time the most important person in my life, the first—and perhaps the only—person ever to treat me as an equal.

Naturally my own troubles preoccupied me at this time, and just as naturally I assumed that older prople always got their own way, but even so I was vaguely aware that things were going from bad to worse for all of us. At night my mother talked about business and hard times. In the store Robert Martin grumbled that the stock wasn't being kept up and customers were being lost. "You have to put the money back into the business," he said. "We need the money to live on," my mother said.

But after a while she decided that she would take a teaching job for us to live on and let the money from the store go back to the store. She had precedent for this, too. Back before I was born, when my father was just putting the store together, he worked nights at the foundry to keep it alive. If he could do it, so could she, and her faith was only sharpened as she recited to me her memory of him coming up the stairs on his hands and knees at the end of his night's work. But all the while some adding machine in her head kept banging out its totals, and when a certain figure showed up, she closed the store instantly. Somehow she had arrived at an estimate of the cash value of the stock that would allow her to satisfy all creditors, and when that figure came around she didn't waste another minute or risk another cent. From that time on, it was the teaching that supported us. But that is by the way.

It was late summer when she closed the store and began to get ready for her new career. Perhaps she wanted to be alone to make her plans and so arranged to ship me off for a bit, or perhaps some friend of my father's, remembering him at last, wanted to make some final gesture of appeasement. In any case, Robert Martin and I found ourselves spending the Labor Day weekend at somebody's camp— my father had friends everywhere, as my mother more than once observed bitterly as she sat in the evening and tried to will cash out of uncollectible accounts.

"Do you know," she said on one such occasion, "that I once saw your father's best suit lying in the gutter outside Hanratty's Saloon? It would have been bad enough if I had been able to pick it up quietly and take it home and clean it, but the town drunk was inside it—that was Billy Farrell, back before the days of Sham Martin, whom you know." (My mother was practicing to be an English teacher.) "I don't think your father ever forgave me for leaving Billy— God rest his soul—there in his disgusting ragged underwear." Nor had he, I might add. Billy had merely lost his pants on that occasion and could be philosophical about having to go home in broad daylight in his long johns, but my father had lost face—or thought he had—and more than once I had heard him tell the story, ostensibly in praise of my mother's strength of character. But I wasn't fooled for a minute, not even I who was fooled by the appearance of everything. I remember this as the first time I was ever aware that there could be a message behind the words, a code I had never suspected.

The camp that Robert Martin and I had for the weekend was on a small pond down in the area we called the Thousand Ponds. It was the pond in back of the pond in back of the pond everyone went to, so it was well back in the woods. In fact, you might have said it was so far in that it was coming out the other side, except that on that side a belt of swamp cut it off from the highway. At some time, not so long before, the water level must have risen and flooded new land—probably there was a dam somewhere in connection with cranberry bogs. I can remember those dead trees standing in the water, silver-white and ghastly, although I'm not sure where the memory comes from, because I am told that I always got down on the floor of the car when we drove along that road.

The pond itself was deep and the water was only slightly brown. There was even a sand beach where we were, which isn't surprising in an area that is all old seabed. But we weren't there for swimming—and I was just as glad, because from time to time out in the middle of the pond we could see backs and tails of truly enormous snapping turtles drifting on the surface like the scalloped spines of ancient monsters—which, I suppose, in a sense they are.

We were floating in a boat in the middle of the pond out where the turtles had been. The turtles were now appearing over near the derelict trees, but I was still somewhat apprehensive in spite of the fact that really I had complete confidence in Robert Martin. He was standing in the boat, casting about, with no luck to speak of, an undersized pickerel and a very big perch, which I would have been glad to catch but which he threw back. Robert seemed to be fishing as well as my father, relaxed, almost negligent, but very skillful. He was, in fact, using my father's rod. I was glad of that. I wanted the rod myself, of course, but had sense enough to know I wasn't ready for it. So I took pleasure in seeing my father's rod and Robert Martin working together so well. I told myself that Robert's casts weren't going quite so far as my father's nor quite so accurately, but really no one could have been sure.

Robert sat down in the boat and rested the rod carefully on the side. He took a flat pint of Scotch whiskey out of his hip pocket, raised it in salute to me, and drank deeply. "Your father, now . . ." he said. I waited. "Your father was a remarkable man." I waited again. Robert took another drink. I think now that he had been working himself up to some kind of funeral oration. Perhaps my mother had put him up to it. Perhaps it was only his sense of fitness. I concentrated on my float, pretending I had a nibble, because he was clearly at a loss. "Your father . . ." he said again and then went on with a rush. "The first time I really saw your father was in the third grade. Miss Moss was the teacher then."

"She still is," I said. I had good cause to know. She was a tartar and more than once let me know that my father had never been half the trouble I was and that I would never be half the man he was.

"She was young then," Robert Martin said. "God, she was pretty." I kept my doubts to myself. "We would all of us do anything for her. In those days I was a great reader. I could read better and faster than anyone, and I loved to be called on to read aloud. This time I'm talking about, I remember we had a new book we wanted to get at because it was about a cave boy. His name was Bodo. I'll never forget it. The first chapter was 'Bodo's Hammer and Knife.' When Miss Moss asked who would like to read first, I put up my hand and so did your father. She called on him and he began to read. I had never thought much about your father before that, but I can still see him standing side of his desk in his white shirt and brown tie, brown knickers, brown knee stockings. He was holding his book like someone going to sing in church." I had a real nibble this time, but I ignored it and the fish went away.

"I was sick," Robert Martin said, "when your father began to read, because almost the first word was *knife,* and I had read it to myself for practice, and if I had been called on I was going to say *ka-nife.* But your father sailed right through it. I've been pretty embarrassed sometimes in my life first and last, but it's funny that the embarrassment I remember best never really happened except in my own head. *Ka-nife.* I still get hot flashes when I just happen to think of it. Now, *knife,* that's your father."

"Are you sure that's the same old lady Moss?" I said, completely at a loss.

"She was still young in those days," he said. "She hadn't found out yet about boys who say *ka-nife.*"

"I never said *ka-nife* in my life," I said.

"I never said you did," Robert Martin said, and he took another drink from the bottle.

And it was just at that moment that the rod—my father's rod—went into the water. Robert had left the lure dangling just above the surface, and something had taken it suddenly and over went the rod. He was after it so fast that with any luck at all he must have caught it before it sank very far. But he came up without it, and no amount of diving produced it. Finally he climbed into the boat over the stern after directing me to the proper place for balance. "Effing turtles," he said, and that was all he said. I knew better than to say anything, but offered to row to the camp and he let me. On the way in, he tried the bottle again and found it empty. He looked around for the nearest turtle and hurled the bottle at it, falling short by something like the length of a football field.

He found some old clothes in a closet and got himself dry and then began rummaging in the kitchen cupboards where he found a large bottle of vanilla extract. Although there was at least one more pint of Scotch whiskey that I knew of, he began sipping the vanilla and brightening from moment to moment. "We'd better eat something," he said. "I was counting on fish, but there aren't any fish, so I'll heat up some soup and we can have the sandwiches your mother made up for us." He set up a card table on the porch where it was warm and sunny.

"Sounds good to me," I said. I didn't really like fish anyway, and neither did my father. He used to hate the bones and would always wind up choking and cursing whenever my mother served fish.

"I would have been mad at your mother—if it was all right to be mad at her—for making sandwiches and showing that she didn't believe we could catch enough fish to eat, but I guess she was right."

"We'll catch plenty this afternoon," I said.

"Plenty and to spare," Robert Martin said. And he told me about the time my father and two other men drank up all the beer while the rest were out fishing. And the time my father's father broke a scab's jaw during a strike at the foundry.

"Now," Robert Martin said, "I'll tell you something nobody else knows. While your father was alive, he and I knew it, and it was really up to him to tell it or not. I don't mind telling it now—speaking only good of the dead, you know." He was deep into his bottle of vanilla now, and he smelled lovely and seemed to be his old self again.

"He and I were fishing in the surf way down on the Cape—at Nauset—your father, I mean—just the two of us. We had a big fire going on the beach. I could show you the place. There was an old wreck there, and I expect some timbers are still sticking out of the sand. It was a lovely night. We had some coffee going and plenty of whiskey. There was a big moon and a strong tide, and everything was just right. Of course your father was getting married in about a week and we couldn't count on many more such nights, but we were trying not to think about that. You know what I mean?" Fortunately he didn't wait for an answer, because I didn't have the remotest idea what he meant except that it was sad to think of the end of such marvelous nights.

"It was around midnight that your father hooked something big. It was fighting hard, and we could see it rolling white on the surface out a ways. I remember thinking, by God, he's really done it this time. He had a hard time of it and was sweating like a horse, but he kept on bringing it in. I was down the beach and up to my waist in the breakers— more than once I was knocked down and nearly swept away. But I had the gaff ready and was all set to jam it home when I saw that what he had caught was a woman. The line was wrapped around her wrist.

"We got her out on the beach and stood looking at her, naked as a fish, because we thought she was dead. Then she opened her eyes and sat up and began laughing. Hysterics, you'll say. But it wasn't that. I've seen enough hysterics in my time to know what's what. No, it wasn't hysterics." He glared at me a moment. "Not at all," he said. "It was a good long, loud laugh.

" 'It's plain to see,' she said, 'that a person born to be hanged is just wasting her time trying to drown herself.'

" 'That was a foolish thing to try, anyway,' your father said.

" 'That's for me to say,' she said. 'But now that you've caught me what are you going to do with me?'

" 'There is that,' your father said. 'What can I do with you?' he said.

"I was over building up the fire to warm her, but I could hear it all. None of us had yet thought of one of the blankets for her, so she just sat there with her long hair stuck to her body and nothing else on her except for the seaweed wrapped around her legs that made her fall back down when she tried to stand up. The seaweed, I remember, was just the color of her hair, rich glossy brown like new-opened horse chestnuts.

" 'What can I do?' your father said.

" 'That's for you to say,' she said.

" 'Well,' your father said. He scratched his head. 'I was going to get married next week anyway, and I suppose I might as well marry you.'

" 'Truly?' she said.

" 'True as I'm standing here,' your father said.

" 'How will you tell her you're marrying me and not her?' she said.

" 'Nothing of the sort,' your father said. 'I'll marry the both of you.' And she began laughing again. 'I'll need some laughter in my life,' he said. 'That's a good woman I'm marrying but dead serious.'

" 'Then how will you tell her you're marrying the both of us?' she said.

" 'That's for me to know,' your father said, 'but she has had her mind set on marrying me since we were in the seventh grade and she couldn't change her mind now whatever I did.'

" 'Then that's how it is,' she said.

" 'That's how it is,' your father said. 'Now take this coffee to warm you and this blanket to hide yourself in, and we'll have some hot fish in a minute, and all will go well as a marriage bell.'

"And so, by God, it did," Robert Martin said.

"Is that really how it happened?" I said. Oh, I was the solemn one.

"I've just told you so, haven't I?" he said.

"But truly," I said. I was bouncing around on my little camp stool, and in my excitement I fell over backward and brought my feet up under the table and sent the soup and sandwiches flying every which way. I felt like an idiot and looked quickly at Robert Martin, expecting to be told I was one, but he was laughing so hard he had to lower himself to the floor to keep from falling too.

"If you don't kill me with laughing," he said, "I'll live to tell your sons about the time their father kicked the lunch over the house and killed the big snapping turtle."

"I'd like to hear that story," I said, still flat on my back.

Unfortunately, I'll never hear that story now, because it was only that winter or the next one that they found Robert Martin in his own net under the thin clear ice of a night. Boys skating peered into the hole and finally saw something that justified all their peering, although at first they thought it was only some weird reflection in the ice. Thank God I wasn't one of them. I see him still, standing beside the hole, gently scattering oatmeal to attract the little fishes.

Living with Snakes

Death is in the garden
Waiting till you pass
For the cobra's in the drain pipe
And the krait is in the grass.
　　　　—RUDYARD KIPLING

When Peter Watts moved into Indiana Price's house, the ground rules were explicit. He would have a room in the house, a Federal house near the village out the river road. He would be a presence in the house for her young son while she was traveling. She traveled a lot. She consulted. She moved and she shook. A son—after all, well, you don't exactly like to leave him at the vet's. And there would be no sex. She wanted the arrangement to last. She had theories about that. Statistics bore her out. Her own experience bore her out: there are some things you just don't try to mix. Living arrangements and sex, for example. She wanted someone who would stay. Someone her son could get used to. Someone he might even watch and learn from. Male role models—Peter winced at that—were hard to come by but very necessary, especially about twelve—John had just turned twelve.

Peter's heart went out to this boy he had not yet seen. If there was one thing he knew, that was what it was like to be a chicken with no chance to peck up gravel for his crop, noth-

ing to chew with. Of course, never having had models himself, having always seen power in the hands of women, he felt
like a fraud in this new light. Shall the blind lead the blind?
But perhaps he and the boy could teach each other. The
whole thing terrified him, but he thought he would try it.

And he was glad he did. With the situation clear between
him and Indiana, it was as if they had gone through sex and
come out the other side. As if they were waking up together
in the morning and it was time to begin to tell her who he
was. To pour it all out to her. To account for all the years
they had not been together.

He felt this from the first moment they sat together in the
room she assigned him. It was a lovely room, the room he
had chosen secretly but had been afraid to request. Its win-
dows opened on fields that ran down to the river. Inside, it
had the look of a study with a desk and bookcases and best
of all a fireplace. She had built a fire that first day and they
sat in front of it and drank herb tea and ratified the terms.

He reached far back beyond the things he had told his
wife when they were first married, beyond the things his
mother knew, to things he had never told anyone, stretching
and reaching for things he didn't even know himself, striv-
ing for something to offer her, something absolutely pure
and untouched, something just for her, just from him. It
was truly that moment of openness that usually comes in
bed the first time after sex is safely behind, that moment of
desire for perfect sharing, before the sediment of doubt and
evasion silts it all up. He thought they would go on from
vision to dazzling vision. He was beside himself with
delight.

And then, almost at once, he began to despair of the con-
tract he had so gladly assumed. For one thing, except at
meals, he saw little of John, who was a studious boy and
kept to his room, doing his homework and reading books
about the Bermuda Triangle, UFO's, and the lives of in-

ventors. Sometimes late at night when the house had gone all still, Peter would hear John's radio, which was never turned off, playing softly upstairs. At first he thought John had a woman in his room—by that hour of the night Peter was usually overtired and not strictly accountable for his impressions. And if the mother had her lovers in, why shouldn't the twelve-year-old son? The mother was very big on openness, on equality, on the personness of all persons.

It was on the nights the lovers came that Peter heard the radio, that he lay awake and tried to cry to relieve the pressure in his throat. Sometimes he slipped out of the house and took long walks along the levee. Sometimes he planned to smash the radio. Sometimes he was able to cry. It was quite clear that he had not got beyond sex at all. Sleep, however, knit it all up, and there was only another day with Indiana—or without her if she was off again. In some ways it was better when she was off.

The next surprise was that Indiana suddenly went against her own dictum and let a lover move into the house, mixing sex and living arrangements. During this time Peter repeatedly left the house in the night with the intention of never coming back. But once he had walked himself into a stagger and finally into a standstill, he turned around. Where was he going anyway?

It would still be winter dark when he let himself back into the house, but all along the valley he had seen lights coming on in bedrooms and kitchens and barns, and he had heard from across the river the sound of tractors starting, the warning clang of heavy equipment creeping backwards through the dark. Then he slept, slept far into the day. The fiction was that he had been reading late.

The lover's name was Francis Moreton. He was called Fran, and he had very long hair and a very long beard and very dirty feet. Of course he went barefoot all the time, so his feet were bound to get dirty. But they not only got dirty, they stayed dirty as long as anyone knew him. He was also a very young man. Younger, of course, than Peter, younger even than Indiana. Not so much older than John when you came right down to it. Peter wondered, in fact, how a man so young could have such a long beard. He must have begun growing it in his cradle, must have been dedicated, like Samson, never to know scissors or razor, a Nazarite before the Lord, destined to mangle monsters and strangle snakes. Or was that Hercules? Or did it matter?

And Fran Moreton had snakes. He had cages and cages of snakes. He had boa constrictors. He had rat snakes. He had milk snakes. He had king snakes. He seemed to have all the snakes that ever were. He stacked the cages in a little room upstairs, an old sewing room. Peter was never able to determine if Indiana knew about the snakes in advance.

A Dutch woman from Java once told Peter that when she was a child cobras lived under the veranda. It was bad luck to kill them. He shuddered and supposed it was even worse luck not to. A man he knew used to kill garter snakes in his garden, apologetically, but he didn't want his children to be frightened when they got into the house, and they would get into the house. He himself had once dealt with—or failed to deal with—a large brown and white snake in the attic of the place in Maine. He was about to put his hand on a patch of mottled attic light as he came up the stairs. The patch flickered, writhed, and vanished under the eaves. He never told anyone. It would catch mice, he assured himself. Surely, he said, it was less dangerous than the bees in the chimney, honey oozing down the walls. Less dangerous than the wasps in the outhouse. But the truth is that he was afraid. It was a mystery, and he was afraid of sacrilege. That was just what it was. And at the end of *Pather Panchali*, a snake crawls in across the threshold of the now-deserted house. A powerful symbol, as an Indian student once explained, of a snake crawling into a deserted house. Desolation.

"But," Peter said, "you said—"

"I know," Indiana said. "It's against what I've always said, but it feels right."

Having lived all his life up to that time in the grip of principles, Peter was but newly turned on to feelings. To be sure, he had always been one to quote Cummings's "since feeling is first, who pays any attention to the syntax of things will never wholly kiss you." But that was all very theoretical with him. He didn't know what he was talking about, having in his life never kissed anyone at all, so to speak. So when Indiana said it felt right, Peter said, Yea, verily, although he didn't have the least idea what she meant. His old accustomed systems were flashing SELF-IN-DULGENCE SELF-INDULGENCE. But he was determined to pay no attention to them. There was a new way—whatever it was—of seeing things, of feeling them. Verily, he said, and amen.

"Is this where I say 'right on'?" Peter said.

"That's not your style," Indiana said.

"Thank you," Peter said. "I couldn't have said it anyway."

"Just say what you think," she said.

"Well," he said in the face of this wholly novel idea, "I assume you know what you're doing." He was really thinking that—among a great many other things.

"Thank you," she said. "I think I do—on some instinctive level. I mean, it feels right."

Peter had an inkling then of what it meant to feel something. He didn't trust it of course, because he was so unused to regarding feelings. But it seemed to him that something was telling him that what Indiana felt was right was, in fact, very wrong.

"Fantastic," she said when Fran moved the cages in.

"How come so many snakes?" Peter said, trying to think of something not too stupid to say.

"I dig snakes," Fran said.

That first night, Fran held an indoctrination meeting. He let them handle the snakes. John was tentative at first but became more confident as he went on. Indiana was enthusiastic from the beginning. Mind over matter, Peter repeated to himself, but he let the others go first, and he quickly faded out of the receiving line.

Then Fran fed one of the boa constrictors. He took a white mouse out of his pocket and put it into the snake's cage. The snake was not particularly interested. The mouse smoothed its fur.

"My mother always believed," Peter said, "in wearing good underwear in case she got run over by a streetcar."

The others looked at him oddly.

Then the snake began to stir itself. Peter drifted into the background. He got heads between himself and the cage. This was a very different matter from an optical illusion in the attic devouring imaginary mice. The others leaned into the cage like bubbles at the edge of the vortex in the bathtub drain.

"Fascinating," Indiana said. Or at least Peter supposed it was Indiana. John's voice, however, was very unreliable at about that time.

After that night Fran Moreton was seldom seen in the house. He had the room next to the snake room, and he stayed there all the time. He never came to meals, so he never shared in the cooking rotation. He seemed to live on Pepsi-Cola and potato chips. "He goes out for pizza sometimes," Indiana said. "Of course he's a night person." She seemed to think that explained everything and conferred some great though vague distinction.

Peter preferred to make his own observations and deductions. He heard quart Pepsi-Cola bottles rumble across the floor sometimes. He found pizza boxes in the trash. Sometimes Fran's door was mysteriously ajar. The floor was littered with gaudy paperbacks. Perhaps a dirty foot showed at the end of the unmade bed. Once when Peter had to check Fran's room for a leak—where was Fran that day?—he saw that the paperbacks were covered with spaceships and monsters. Galaxies and mystic symbols. Books slipped beneath his feet. Bottles clinked and jostled. In the night sometimes Peter heard Fran's bare feet slithering in the halls and on the stairs, pervading the house, passing all the doors.

Silent as Fran normally was, however, he was a very noisy lover. He groaned and he bellowed. "Shit, piss, fuck," he shouted. Not a sound from Indiana. "Say it," he shouted. "Say it. Tell it like it is." Not a sound. "Cunt," he said.

Peter, lying rigid in his bed, thought of John lying rigid upstairs over him. Perhaps he slept through it, though. Perhaps he was safe.

John wasn't safe, of course, but it wasn't the love cries that threatened him. At least Peter could see no sign of that. No, it was something very different, and it began quite simply.

"Fran hasn't fed the snakes lately," John said. "It's way past time."

"Really?" Peter said.

"I've been reading up on it," John said. "I've asked at the pet shop."

"I'm sure he knows what he's doing," Peter said, and he let it go.

"I suppose he does," John said. "He ought to anyway."

That night, however, when Peter heard Fran slide out of the house, stalking a pizza no doubt, he went cautiously into the snake room. He looked at each of the snakes, but he could tell nothing. They behaved very much like snakes. They were either completely still or they rolled slowly over their own coils. Their steady eyes watched him. Their nervous tongues tested the air.

He lay awake for a long time waiting for Fran to come

back. He would sleep, he thought, when the last flame of his fire flickered out. But he didn't sleep. When the checkered log finally went black. When the blackened log at last broke and fell from the andirons.

He woke with a start and lay rigid as Fran's feet hissed past his door, past Indiana's door, up the stairs, past John's door. A door shut firmly. Clicked shut. A bottle rolled. And all was quiet. It occurred to Peter then that it had been a long time since he heard Fran shrieking the obscenities of love, since he had himself lain awake alternately listening and putting his hands over his ears, straining to hear and dreading to hear, angry, indignant, despairing. At least this was better for John, he thought, or thought he thought.

Two days later John said, "He still hasn't fed them. I don't know what to do. Perhaps I could buy some mice myself. I have a little money—"

"I'll speak to him," Peter said. Now he would have to do it. He was very unhappy, for once a little displeased with John.

Nevertheless, that night he settled in the kitchen to make bread. Fran would have to pass him to get out, but it was very late before he heard Fran's stealthy rustle on the hall matting. "Oh, hello," Peter said, looking up from his book. "I decided to make some bread."

"Hello," Fran said. He never ceased to flow toward the door.

"Smells good, doesn't it?" Peter said.

"Uh," Fran said as if bread was not at all among his interests—but then what was?

"Anything wrong with the snakes?" Peter said. "John says you haven't fed them."

"It's OK," Fran said. And he slipped out the door.

"What about Fran?" Peter said to Indiana in the morning as they set up their day.

"What about him?" Indiana said. "He's a very odd

young man." She sounded as if Fran were someone she barely knew, a crackpot of dubious reputation.

"He's not feeding the snakes," Peter said. "John and I are worried. We think maybe we'd better get some mice. John knows what to do."

"We can't interfere," Indiana said.

"He's crazy," Peter said.

"We mustn't interfere," Indiana said. "They're his snakes."

"But he's killing them," Peter said.

"There's nothing we can do."

But John insisted there was everything they could do, and Peter for once sided against Indiana. He bought mice at the pet shop and secretly brought them home.

"He's put a lock on the door," John said. "Why is he doing this?"

"I don't know," Peter said. Having committed himself to an action against all his habits of noninvolvement, he felt the more bitterly frustrated. He was ready to assert himself. He was ready to act. And he was very simply prevented. The unaccustomed exertion was nearly proving too much for him.

Still, the next day Peter waited until he was alone in the house—or thought he was alone. It was more and more difficult to know where Fran was. He had gone very quiet in his room. If he ever left it at all, it must have been when they were all away. He must have lain there straining to hear, listening for doors, for cars starting. He must have tried to piece together scraps of overheard plans—Peter knew all about that. He was totally silent. He was totally invisible.

Peter went out into the yard and climbed the big old maple on that side of the house. Even as a boy, tree-climbing had terrified him, and now he climbed in thorough terror and in anger. He could see into the snake room. The snakes were quiet in their cages. What had he expected? No big branch went close to the house. If he was going to try the window at all, he would have to use a ladder.

He shifted his gaze to Fran's window. Fran was watching him. His hair and beard were wild as a prophet's. He stood in the attitude of denunciation. His lips moved silently. Peter clung to the tree for dear life and then, slowly, trembling, made his way to the ground.

"You've got to tell him he can't do this," Peter said to Indiana.

"There's nothing I can do about it," Indiana said.

"You've got to tell him he can't do this in your house," Peter said.

"He's got to do what he's got to do," Indiana said.

Peter was speechless. That's crazy, he said to himself. He knew he should have said it to her, and he was ashamed. You can't do this to John, he should have said. You can't do this to us. You can't do this to me. To me. To me. And I've got to do what I've got to do, he should have said. But he had no idea what that was.

When he woke up in the morning, however, a voice in his head was saying, I shall get a ladder. I shall break the window. I shall have a box of mice. If he tries to stop me, I shall kill him.

Peter was used to these voices. He had had them all his life off and on. They spoke to him in the morning usually, when he was still not quite awake. Sometimes they told him the answer to a problem that had been bothering him. Sometimes they spoke the proper form of a sentence he hadn't been able to find. Lately there had been an aged Indian, a blind prophet of his people. The Indian spoke to him morning after morning about the spells and incantations he sang for his people. Spells for buffalo and spells for fish. Rain spells. And spells against a hard winter. Prepare, oh, prepare, was his song, and it was good. He lived among his people, loved and tended, his flesh warmed at night by young women who whispered of lovers when they thought he was asleep. He dreamed himself, a woman's dream, of a lover who lived in the forest, wooed but elusive, a lover named Death. I am an old man, the Indian sang, I live in my daughter's house. Droplets of life seep under my door. I take them up on blotting paper and sniff them while I lie awake. The Indian was a sweet old man, and Peter was making a book of his sayings.

It was not, of course, the Indian who spoke to Peter that morning, although the Indian had often enough referred to stealing the strength of men he had killed. This was a new voice, an alarming voice, a dangerous voice that threatened and promised at the same time, the two sides of a coin that could be spent only once. I'll kill him, Peter said in his own voice, and sprang out of bed.

"Don't tell me about it," Indiana said.

"All right," Peter said, "I won't."

"I can feel it," Indiana said. "You radiate it. It's all wrong and I want no part of it."

"You shall have no part of it," Peter said. He felt like a rock in a frost, solid and hard but full of water ready to explode him.

"It's an invasion of privacy," Indiana said. "It's a violation of integrity."

"It's puking-up sick," Peter said, "and it's gone far enough."

"I can't stand it," Indiana said. And she walked away.

Peter was astonished. It was natural law with him that Indiana could stand anything. All the water in his rock froze at once, and he was as dust. But he was left with a box of mice in his room, with a ladder laid ready, with a hatchet to break the pane near the window lock, with heavy gloves to reach through the jagged hole. It was this same hatchet he would use to kill Fran Moreton when he burst into the room.

For days now Peter had worked on his plan. His plan was ready. He had waked up with full resolution to carry it out. And now he collapsed. Even in defying Indiana he had counted on her equal resolution. He had exulted in his decision. Now that she proved as fragile as he, he was at a loss. He had never expected this.

It happened, however, that the plan had a life of its own. Just sitting in the kitchen, drinking coffee, and sending John off to school and Indiana off to work had always been the first step. "Have a good day," he said to Indiana. "Good luck on your test," he said to John. "Hope you make the team." John wanted to play basketball. Peter really wanted him to play. He wanted to watch him and gloat. But at the same time he knew it was a step apart. He saw John with less time for walks and talks. He saw, say, a coach touching John's mind, touching, shifting, diverting. He saw John moving away, opening out, and he saw himself never again going anywhere.

He began his morning routine as soon as the others had left. He pulled on his heavy gloves to carry up the wood for the fireplaces, and he used his little hatchet to split some kindling. He laid Indiana's fire carefully and then his own—he had built up the kitchen fire before anyone else was up. But then with the gloves and the hatchet to hand, he was so far into the imagined plan that he went on without really willing it.

The aluminum ladder was light and easy. He looked out carefully for electric wires near the window, although he had scouted the area a dozen times in advance. The mouse box went into a pack he strapped tightly to his back. He went up the ladder slowly with his hatchet in his hand. It must have been like this when his Indian scaled the palisades at Deerfield. He tapped the glass with the back of the hatchet and reached in for the lock. It was all so easy.

Then he was in the room waiting. There was no sound from the next room. There was no sound in this room. The snakes lay still in their cages. They were very like snakes. But they were dead. It was only then that he became aware of the smell. He put his head out the window and threw up.

He tossed the hatchet out the window. It split the earth without a sound. He crept down the ladder even more slowly than he had gone up. Retrieved the hatchet. Passed through the kitchen. Through the hall. Past Indiana's door and past his own. His eyes felt red and fierce. He was completely noiseless on the stairs. Even the steps that always groaned were now silent. His blood was thudding in the back of his skull—unless it was Fran's blood, bleeping and listening, bleeping and listening.

Fran's door latch was silent, the same latch Peter listened for in the night, its small shriek, its snap on its secret. And the door eased open on an empty room.

The floor was covered with empty potato-chip bags, an old trick Peter knew. He had read of it and even practiced it himself when he stopped at dubious hotels. No one could have taken a step in that room without an uproar of paper. Or without a clatter of bottles—not a trick Peter had read of but one he appreciated at once. A barrier reef of paperbacks in toppled piles outlined the bed. The bed itself was unmade, the sheets gray. Fran had somehow slipped out and vanished.

Peter faced the door of the snake room. He smashed at the lock with the back of the hatchet. The sharp click echoed through the house. It echoed through Peter and released the force for a greater blow. He had never smashed at anything like that before except wood. The lock sprang open. He turned aside. He was not yet ready to open that door.

He went down the stairs. Every tread now groaned as it knew how to do. He must find a shovel and dig a hole, a deep hole in the garden, down into the winter earth, black loam on his boots, among old roots of things and sleeping bulbs, memorabilia, and the silt of ten thousand floods.

The First Baseman

She had long dark hair that she pulled straight back and tied with a piece of bright, heavy yarn. It gave her face a forward-straining, eager look—something like a figurehead, very, very quiet. Just the same there was nothing wooden about her. Although her expression rarely changed—as far as I can remember, she never smiled—she was simply relaxed and alert. I assumed she was intelligent as well. I also assumed she was gentle, compassionate, and very loving. I was, of course, madly in love with her. And the first time I stood beside her I realized she was fully six-foot-two in her baseball shoes.

I'm an even six-foot myself—well, although it's not generally known, five-foot-eleven and fifteen-sixteenths inches. That sticks in my craw because I always wanted to be six-foot, and I've been led to lie a lot about it.

Every night after work I was out at the softball park, hoping her team would be playing. I got into the habit of hanging around the refreshment stand to buy her a beer after the games. Each night she looked mildly down at me and thanked me and drank her beer. The next night I would be back in the stands with the odd husband, a boyfriend or two, a scattering of babies. The center fielder on her team—great arm, strong and accurate—used to leave her baby on a bench there bundled up in one of those things Indian women use, a carrying board of some kind, and when she wasn't in the field or at bat she would whip out a breast and feed it.

My first baseman was marvelous. She played as good a first base as I have ever seen, very close to the bat, more than halfway down the line, crouched, ready, arms hanging, weight just balanced. I really worried about her playing so far in. In cricket there are positions very close to the bat called silly mid-on and silly mid-off. Well, she played a silly first base, but she was very quick. Great hands. The greatest. I've seen men sit and catch flies with their hands. I even knew a man who could pick them out of the air between his thumb and forefinger. And there is the legendary samurai who could snap them up with chopsticks. I doubt if she had ever heard of chopsticks, but she was in that league.

I came very late to women's softball, but I had watched a lot of baseball—I'm a frustrated first baseman myself. That is, I was slow to react and couldn't hit. Anything else? But I know what is good just the same, and she had it all. She could hit. She could run. When she stood up to an umpire, it was her jaw she stuck out, not her chest, although I had checked that statistic, too, of course. But when I watched her play I only thought exactly what I thought when I watched Joe DiMaggio: Christ, how beautiful. Perhaps all the time I had been wanting to be in love with a really great first baseman and didn't know it.

Well, I bought her a beer—I swear it—just the same way I would have bought a beer for Joe DiMaggio if he had really been there and willing to accept a beer. I think I did anyway. It's hard to tell for sure. I did think it over. I thought it over long after I knew she went to the refreshment stand after every game. I asked myself: Look now, if this was Joe DiMaggio would you buy him a beer if he was really here? Or is it that buying a beer is what you do for a woman?

The next night I bought a beer for the winning pitcher in

a game in the men's league. He was in the executive training program of the bank where I cash my checks and just about the only person in town I know. A couple of nights after that I bought one for the third baseman on the Indian team. He had done something I admired—envied actually. He was playing way in with a runner on third and fielded a hard smash perfectly and faked a throw to first. The runner broke for home and was tagged out before he could stop. It was really great.

And then I said to my first baseman, "Can I buy you a beer? You had a great game." It seemed just right. I couldn't see a thing wrong with it. Actually, there was supposed to be one more step after I bought the beer for the Indian third baseman. I wanted to test my feelings by buying for someone on the Indian women's team. That team was, after all, my first love. I went night after night to see them play. They were all fat and jolly, and I enjoyed their games because they enjoyed them so, even their own strikeouts, their own errors. But when it came right down to action, I couldn't buy any one of them a beer. It wasn't only that I couldn't find one of them to tell she had a great game. There was also the matter of a sneaking doubt that even if I could buy her a beer I wouldn't dare buy a beer for a white woman. I didn't want to know that. Then when I discovered that I could in fact buy a beer for my first baseman, I was no longer interested in buying a beer for anyone else.

"Thanks," she said. She raised the can to me. I raised mine to her. I never was one for small talk. That accounts for a lot, I suppose—accounts for the fact that we went on the same way for about a month. And I swear when I watched her play, it was as if she truly was Joe DiMaggio. When I saw her in the post office, though, it was different.

Each morning on the way to work I checked my mailbox. I had noticed her in there picking up mail for some office. She wore a jacket and mini-skirt I recognized after a while as the uniform of the tellers at my bank. She was impressive all right, but I didn't think much about her until I saw her play. Then I began to time my visits to the post office more carefully. My day would be off to a very bad start if I didn't see her squat and open the big bank box on the lowest level of boxes. The splendor of her thighs in nylon—which I never thought about when I saw them bared on the field—the swell of her breast when she reached through the box to pick up the canvas pouch from the floor—oh, I was nearly out of my mind. I couldn't tell if I was in love with a first baseman or a woman. Curiously, we never spoke in the post office. We avoided each other's eyes. I never said, "I dreamed of your plays." It wasn't strictly true anyway. I just lay awake and reran the entire game and bits of other games as well, but it was as good as dreaming.

At the end of a month of beers she said, "You're quite a fan, aren't you?" She leaned back against the counter with both elbows. I couldn't have been more pleased if she had shot a stream of tobacco juice at a passing rat.

"Oh, yes," I said. "I wouldn't miss a game."

"What will you do now the season is over?"

That was something I had been trying not to know. The thought had crossed my mind from time to time, but I had managed pretty well to assume that the season would go on forever. "Buy a TV, I guess," I said.

"There'll be basketball," she said, "but that's a long way off."

"What will you do?" I said.

"Run after work," she said. "Allow myself an extra beer."

"Does that start now?" I said. I made a slight gesture with my can.

"Training is now relaxed," she said. It was as near to a smile as I ever saw on her face.

"Well—" I said.

"They're closing up now," she said. And we had to step forward to avoid being hit by the hatch coming down.

"There are lots of places," I said.

"I can't go dressed like this," she said

I was desperate. "Look," I said. It was all slipping away—what there was of it. "If you were Joe DiMaggio, I'd ask you to my place for a beer."

"But I'm not Joe DiMaggio."

Things were rapidly getting worse. "I mean, you don't know me."

"DiMaggio wouldn't know you either."

She sure wasn't making it easier for me. "I mean, well, you're a woman."

"Yeah," she said.

"I mean, you have to be careful."

"So does DiMaggio," she said. "You might turn out to be some kind of queer."

"Oh, no," I said.

"I said *might*," she said. "But that would make it all right for me to go to your place."

"Yeah," I said. I felt a little sick.

"Or I might not be interested in men—look how big I am."

I must have looked as stunned as I felt.

"I guess you're interested in women," she said. "And I only said *might*. You have to touch all the bases, you know."

That put her one up, because in spite of her *might* I still didn't know if she was interested in men. I wished to hell she had kept quiet. It had never occurred to me in spite of her size and in spite of the way she could make me forget when I watched her play.

"Put up your hand," she said.

I was caught off guard and flung up my hand to ward off a blow.

"No," she said, "like this." She had her elbow resting on the broad shelf of the refreshment stand outside the closed hatch. She wanted to arm-wrestle.

"OK," I said. I put down my elbow and clasped her

hand—it was not at all like clasping a man's hand. Immediately she began to put on pressure. Nothing sudden. Just letting me know she wasn't wasting any time. For a while then she let me build up the tension, and she just held. My arm began to tremble. Then she pressed my arm down. It didn't seem to take a special effort. I couldn't feel a tremor in her arm. Surely there was no change of expression on her face.

I laughed—or tried to. "Step right up and call her Joe DiMaggio," I said.

"Make that Joan," she said. "OK," she said, "now we both know that, let's forget about it, OK?"

"Sure," I said, although it wasn't the kind of thing I was likely to forget.

"Now, do you still want to go to your place for a beer?"

"Oh," I said. "Yeah. Sure."

At the door of my apartment building I noticed that I automatically stepped back so she could go first and that she as automatically went on ahead. She clumped up the stairs in her baseball shoes as if she were on her way to the Yankee locker room. But those tight-ass shorts going on before were a different matter altogether. Those bare legs. On her right thigh there was a large angry scrape where she had slid into second, a picture-book slide. I was about to say I hoped it wasn't too sore—Gee, Joe, that's some raspberry—but I stopped in time. Not that she probably would have minded. In fact, I suppose she would have been more likely to knock me down if I had said something that showed I hadn't been enjoying her legs.

I told her to make herself at home while I went to the kitchen. When I came back with two bottles of beer—I wouldn't have given DiMaggio a glass—she had taken off her spikes and was coiled into my easy chair, very womanly.

"Did you see that play in the third inning?" she said.

"The pick-off?" I said.

"Right."

"She was out," I said.

"She never got back to the bag," she said. "I was back there and took the throw before she got turned around."

"Nice pickup," I said.

"Worst throw she's made all year." Her right hand, hanging over the arm of the chair, made a little scooping motion—she was left-handed, something else I liked about her—and she seemed quite pleased with herself.

"The umpire was out of position," I said.

"He was looking at the shortstop's ass," she said. "The creep. I know him."

"Well, anyway," I said, "now you can sit back and figure your batting average."

"Three eighty-seven," she said.

"Including tonight's game?"

"Sure. I went two for three. I figured it at the bank this afternoon on the machine."

"You mean you really planned two for three?"

"Of course not." She frowned at me. "I figured O for one and one for one and O for two and one for two and two for two. Like that."

"So it was a good season," I said.

"I wanted to break four hundred," she said.

"So did DiMaggio," I said.

"The last four-hundred hitter was Ted Williams," she said.

"Right," I said. "Four-O-six in '41."

"Right," she said. We drank to that and were silent in admiration of the Splendid Splinter.

I couldn't think of any way to go on, so I had to go back. "Jesus Christ never batted four hundred," I said.

"He had a bad year," she said.

"Babe Ruth said that."

"I know," she said, "about the president."

"That was why the Babe made more money than the president," I said. We looked at each other for just a second as if we had exchanged the secret handshake. Then we took small drinks of our beer.

"Did you ever play?" she said at last.

"High school," I said.

"I thought so," she said. "Not since then?"

"I hurt my shoulder," I said. "I can't throw."

"Tough luck," she said.

"I was diving for a shot over the bag—I didn't even get it."

"First base?" she said.

"Right," I said.

"Left-handed?"

"Right," I said. "I mean, yes." We exchanged another small look. "I wouldn't dare play the way you do."

"I've got good reflexes," she said.

"Great hands," I said. She held them up and we both admired them. They were long and slender, very very long fingers. What people call artist's hands. They were lovely and soft looking, and I knew exactly how strong they were.

"What kind of hitter were you?" she said.

"Not much," I said. "I usually managed my hit a game."

"Say two-fifty."

"About that," I said.

"It might have got better if you could have worked on it."

"Oh, sure," I said. "Have another beer?"

"Why not?" she said. I brought the beer. "I work at it all the time. Study films of my swing. Films of great hitters. Williams for one. Around the first of the year I'll start in the batting cage over at the college. Next year is going to be the four-hundred year."

"Right on, brother," I said. She didn't notice, and I didn't either—or at least not much.

We drank all the beer in my refrigerator. Before I could

offer to drive her home, she said, "I'll jog home now. It helps me sleep."

Next morning I fumbled with my mailbox and watched her fill the bank's pouch. Those thighs. Those silken knees. And hands, quick and light and sure, bright red nails. Her loose hair swinging low so that I couldn't see her face. When she stood up she turned the other way and walked briskly out of the post office. Her spike heels very loud on the marble floor.

The Contrivance

Day after day I watched the old man swim. We always swam in the same lanes, side by side, and once we were started we always maintained the same relative positions. Some of that was conscious on my part. I don't know about him.

We would usually arrive at the pool at about the same time and would wait for the door to open. For months we each pretended to be alone. Then finally one of us said something, perhaps about the guard's being late or perhaps about the cold draft in the hall. After that we always had the weather or the hope that the pool wouldn't be too crowded. Never more than that. I spent the time psyching myself up for swimming. I didn't want to be there at all. I wanted a drink and I wanted my supper. But I just stood there and listened to the thud, thud, thud at the base of my skull. I also yawned a lot.

On land he was a brisk, round man who moved with short quick steps. You might almost say he was chubby and plump except that he wasn't really jolly. He didn't have a big white beard either—a thick white mustache, but no beard. If we had ever walked together he would have quickly left me behind, for I have always moved very slowly— walked slowly, swum slowly, and it takes me twice as long to dress as anyone else. Why, the old man could whip into his one-piece BVD's (or long johns), shirt, tie, pants, vest, coat, shoes, rubbers, and be out of the gym while I was still trying to find the right way into my undershirt.

When the lifeguard opened the door—there was a wire mesh at the bottom of the door through which we could see her legs, and they were very nice legs indeed—when she opened the door, we would go to our favorite lanes. I would ease into the water, bracing myself against the corner of the pool. I had hurt my back once diving in, and now I preferred to honor the small yellow sign that said No Diving. Meanwhile, the old man would be exchanging a few words with the guard. She had walked away from us—very nice bathing suits she always had—to open the women's door and then back to her post. I would be tonguing spit into my goggles to keep them from fogging—at least someone once told me that spit keeps them from fogging. And it is important that the glass be clear. For one thing, I think I'm smothering when my goggles fog. For another, I like to do a lot of looking when my face is in the water. Swimming is so boring. I look at the girls as they swim past me—within arm's length—I could almost bite them. Sometimes they kick me as they go past. There was a girl once—she always kicked me. I think she liked me. Lovely red toenails.

But the girls always came late. For ten minutes, a quarter of an hour, sometimes even longer, the old man and I would have the pool to ourselves. And it was the old man I watched. I call him old because he struck me as an old man, although in truth he probably wasn't so much older than I was. But I don't think of myself as old even if I can plainly see that many men my age are old. Even some who are younger are old. But I seem to have got stuck somewhere. I can't assign an age to myself. Somewhere in my prime, though. At my best. Of course I know I'm tired in the evening, unable to do that extra work needed to make a career. Even so, the old man is old and I am not.

I pull my goggles down and take a deep breath. Just then

there is a shattering crash as the old man hits the water. There is no other crash like his. If he is late and I am already settled into my treadmill trance, I know that crash. I check my bearings to learn where to expect to see him coming past. And there he is, stretched effortless in the water, a great pale beast, flippers, tail motionless, gliding. Walrus. Or seal. Or something legendary like manatee or dugong, fading into myth. Or fish, of course, all teeth and fury, seeking what it may devour.

Then it all changes. His legs draw up, his arm reaches—it is a sedate but powerful sidestroke that he does. I do a sort of bastard crawl of my own invention. And like everything I do, it is very slow. I have overheard men in the locker room wondering how I can stay afloat at that rate. But it works out that my crawl and his sidestroke keep us very much together. In fact, he swims marginally faster than I do, but he takes an extra breath or two at the turns. Also he often stops to talk to some girl in the next lane. We get on. I wonder every day how conscious of me he is.

I play a good deal—swimming is so boring—with the idea of the fish, the beast, the monster, the myth, but it is the other aspect, Pose Two, so to speak, that really interests me: knees drawn up, arms reaching. I consult my sources. My arms and legs go on as I have taught them in my own angry way. I don't know whom I am spiting by refusing to learn to swim properly—the doctor who said, "EXERCISE," or myself or this wretched body that threatens mutiny more and more each year. Why, if I were to keep up a constant kick, if I were to get more power into my right arm, if I were to change my rate of breathing, I'd leave that old man so far behind he might as well be a rock instead of a fish, a lighthouse instead of a monster. But as it is, we go on. My face in the water. His knees drawn up. His arm stretching. I review pictures in my head.

There is a room of black Goyas in the Prado. Figures

flying in the clouds. Witches. Demons. There are ceilings in Italy. Angels flying. I can't get a specific ceiling. More the idea of many ceilings. Paintings, too. Did painters study figures in water to guess at the posture of figures in air? Whom to ask? Where to look? Questions that vanish anyway once I'm out of the pool. The shower washes them away along with the chlorine. The warmth eases them out along with the chill, the aches. The water pounds on my back like a long echo.

Swimming, of course, was not the whole of my life. I don't know that the rest was much better, but it would be terrible to hate and resent everything the way I hated and resented swimming. I think there have been times like that, but this was not one of them—or at least so it seems to me now. For one thing, in the midst of all that, my mother came to take a look at me.

All the years of my marriage my mother had refused to visit me, but as soon as my wife ran off "to be happy" my mother appeared to set my life in order. One day my wife told me she wanted some excitement before it was too late. And off she went. And on my mother came.

If a man my age may be old, then a woman my mother's age may certainly be expected to be old. Logically I concede that my mother is an old woman, but actually I don't see it. To be sure, she is white-haired now and seems a little smaller—her doctor ("a lovely young man") put her on a diet years ago, so she is no longer that magnificent Edwardian richness of my dreams. I know all that. But still she goes everywhere and talks to everyone and could, I firmly believe, still knock down an overgrown eighth-grader with her umbrella. Of course that was in the good old days when parents came to thank you for caring so much about their children's future and often brought you a present—a chicken in a burlap bag, a bottle or two of their own wine, a chain of their own sausages. Good things. Good days.

It happened that in the middle of my mother's long-desired, very happy visit I had to go off and leave her for three days—I wonder if the old man at the pool missed me. He never said anything about it, perhaps on the theory that when a person behaves badly it is best to let him see it is of no consequence and therefore not worth repeating. I suspect the old man of all kinds of wisdom.

Anyway, I had to go off to a conference, a very ordinary dull conference that I was attending out of sheer habit. It wouldn't have borne a moment's rational thought. My mother chose, however, to believe I was going off to see a woman.

"What a contrivance," she said. "A conference indeed. I know all about those conferences. Your father's were in Indianapolis."

"Surely you can't get into much trouble in Indianapolis," I said.

"You can get into trouble in Anaheim, Asuza, and Cucamonga," she said. She used to listen to Jack Benny. "You can get into trouble at the A&P."

She was down on her knees imposing order on my wife's borders, weeding, thinning, bringing every plant to attention. They were learning where they were and no mistake. I had told her I'd hire a kid to do all that and she could sit in a chair and supervise, have him move the chair as the sun shifted, bring her a bloody mary or a gin and tonic as the day changed. Her snort of contempt had lost none of its force.

So there she was down on her knees while I shifted from foot to foot and waited for the cab to come and take me to the airport and out of this scene in which "that sweet old lady was working away on her hands and knees while her great hulking shiftless son" and so on with peeping neighbors, adding all my wife's favorite embellishments. They would be right, too. I did have a hasty feeling that "any man who was really a man" would easily and naturally have contrived something better. In truth I was only going to Chicago, a city in which I have never managed to get into any trouble at all.

"This makes me think," she said, "of once when you were small. Your father, God rest his soul, was already dead and I, I'm afraid, had my eye on another man."

"My God," I said. We both rocked back on our heels, I figuratively and she literally, on her knees resting back on her heels.

"You're old enough now," she said. "Don't act so shocked."

"I'm not," I said. But I was. I was completely stunned. "I'm glad." I knew what I was supposed to say, what good men say in books. But all my life I had admired her devotion to my father's memory. Of course she always said, "Never again with any man." But I hadn't taken that at face value. She was the widow Reade, as we used to say. She was my mother.

"We're both too old to be playing games," she said.

"Of course," I said. Her head was tipped back, her face lifted to me, but I couldn't see her eyes under the brim of her big gardening hat. At least she wouldn't be able to see my eyes either.

"It was very early in the morning," she said. "You were asleep. My mother was coming down on the interurban trolley to look after you for the day—do you remember the interurbans?"

"Of course," I said. "I remember the open-sided cars in the summer, and the wait on a siding in a field for the other car to pass. I remember putting apples on the tracks and sometimes pennies and at least once rocks. The Little Man was very angry with us—that was the conductor. He had a bushy white mustache—"

"That was Mr. Brown," my mother said.

"He always waved to us. He made us take the rocks off before he would go on."

"You might have derailed the car," my mother said. "That would have been all I needed."

"That was another day," I said.

"There I was all set to run for the train the minute your grandmother showed up, and there you were derailing her car."

"I was asleep," I muttered. "You said I was asleep."

"I can do without help like that," my mother said. She seemed angry, as if the rocks were still on the tracks and her mother was still kept from arriving and I was still hiding behind the lilac bush. "I was supposed to be getting out of there to please my mother—she wanted me out of the way. And that suited me fine. Do you remember the trains?"

"Of course I remember the trains," I said. "There was the day train and the night train."

"I was taking the 7:15 to Boston," she said.

"The day train was the afternoon freight and the night train brought the men back from Boston in time for supper. I remember all that."

"I was so nervous I was ready to jump out of my skin," she said.

"There must have been a train in the morning," I said, "but I never saw that."

"Of course you did," my mother said. "You went in town with me time after time. You cashed in the ticket stubs in the South Station."

"I remember that," I said.

"The man I was going to meet—" my mother said.

"You don't have to tell me this," I said.

"—was someone you never knew."

"There was a nursery along the track somewhere on the way to Boston," I said. It was suddenly clear before me.

"I thought seriously at one time of marrying him."

"MacGregor's Nursery, it was called. I always looked for Mr. MacGregor, and once I even thought I saw Peter Rabbit.

"I was ready to run off in the other direction the minute I saw my mother step off the trolley, but I was so nervous that I began pulling weeds from my border—that was what made me think of all this. All in my Sunday best, I was pulling weeds, and my mother was standing there before I knew it.

" 'Scoot,' my mother said. 'Study hard.' I had told her I was taking a course at BU, so—no, I wasn't in my best. I had some things in a little bag disguised as books. I was going to change in the South Station—I did change in the South Station. I was full of contrivances."

"I'm going to call the cab again," I said. "I'm getting worried." But fortunately at that moment the cab pulled into the drive. I waved to the driver. He honked anyway, jealous of his rights.

"Study hard," my mother said. I wanted to tell her that a conference wasn't like that, but I wasn't sure exactly what it was like. The taxi honked again.

Sometime before I went to Chicago, the old man didn't show up at the pool for a week. I worried about him. I needn't have. Suddenly he was there again, standing at the door of the pool, striking it with the side of his fist. Thud, thud, thud. "I like the echo," he said. Later that day I overheard him telling the guard that he had been in Washington advising the Senate about atomic energy. That kind of old man. I wanted more than ever to say something to him, something that would make him smile and take a second look at me. But what do you say to an old man who instructs the Senate on the way it is? *The guard is late,* you say. You say, *Unseasonably hot/cold/wet/dry weather we're having.* You say, when the light is flicked on in the pool and shines through the grill at the bottom of the door—you say, *What light through yonder window breaks?* And he says right back, *It is the east, and Juliet is the sun.*

That's nice in a way, of course, but it's also depressing. He knows the responses to my lines, but if he were to start it himself I wouldn't know what to say at all. He might say, *What atomic phenomenon is revealed through the interstices of that ferrous grid—slightly oxidized, of course?* I might say, πr^2 or H_2SO_4. But although the formulas have stuck, I've forgotten what they mean—if I ever knew. *Great legs,* I say as she pauses to unlock the door. He says, *I'd know them anywhere.* And she opens the door. Says, *Hi,* over her shoulder and goes off to open the women's door. Orange bathing suit today.

After that I didn't worry when he was missing. But I wondered. He went to Russia. He went to China. Yugoslavia. Hawaii. And while he was away I tried for self-improvement. But it is a very resistant self.

Face down in the pool, I do fractions. One thirty-sixth. One-eighteenth. One-twelfth. One-ninth. Five thirty-sixths. I hate it. Legs already aching. Feet on the edge of cramps. It will pass. One-sixth. Breathing isn't right. I think I'm smothering. Fuck it all. Nothing is worth this. Every day I hate it. Seven thirty-sixths.

She passes me on the turn—two-ninths. I can't see her. I can't hear her with my cap over my ears. But I know she is there. She passes me every six lengths. And it is time. If only I ever learned to swim faster I could swim up her crotch and bite her ass. Theoretically. Before we got used to each other in the water we often brushed as we passed. She has kicked me all over first and last. I know the accidental feel of her thigh. We have blushed and stammered. Now we know each other, we never speak. My fingers remember her thigh. Do her toes remember my head? Water up my nose. Pay attention. Pay attention.

Goggles steam up. At least I don't have to look up her

crotch as she churns past me. Very nice legs. Built like a weasel. Otter. Even that will pass. Swim every fucking day and it will still pass. She'll see. She says, *Of course.* But she doesn't believe it. One-sixth. Can't be at this end of the pool. Seven thirty-sixths. Cough-groan. I can make the muscles go on. I can make the lungs behave. Once again she goes past me in a storm of white water.

My father. I see him in the snow. He is often just there. Near the five white birch trees on the little mound. The rough cart path crosses the face of the hill and descends to the pond. We slide. He has come out with us to slide. He is very glad. He is glad to be there with his boy. He runs with the sled and belly-flops on the icy slope. He goes very fast and might set a record out on the pond, but he veers into the birches. Crash. He stands there. His back is hurt. Oh, he is so angry. So hurt. He stands there. He is no longer glad. He leaves the sled. He leaves his boy. He limps home, betrayed by his back. How could I know? But I remember.

I'm driving now. Driving muscles. Driving breath—what about heart? OK. All quiet. Already twenty years older than my father ever was. Lungs, goddamn it, a black mess. I'm swimming through a sea of his cigarette butts thrown from the boat as we fish. Turn and breathe. Face down and stroke and bubble and turn and breathe. Like clockwork. What fucking great lungs. And heart. Not a stutter. Not a stammer. Not a single goddamned pound. Must be a fucking third by now. Easy. Be fair. Guess low when you lose count. A third. Twelve goddamned thirty-sixths.

She doesn't know about snow. She thinks all pools are heated and that you'll never bump down the last bit of hill to the pond and float out over the ice easy. So easy. Someone skids a stone past you and it rings over the ice, a wild and melancholy moan. She doesn't know how cold it is on the ice, in the snow, there where five white birches crowd the turn, where the ice is too slick for your runners to catch. She just doesn't know. Was I looking back to a third or ahead to a third? Even otters get their asses bitten. Their lungs go black. They lose a breast. The other breast. They're in snow up to their asses. She goes by me again in the water. I swim through her wake, through a sea of white bubbles. I reach. Reach. But she is gone. By the time she slows down I'll be dead.

I knew an otter once. Wrong end for a third. Has to be thirteen thirty-sixths. Thirteen is prime. Unlucky, but prime. She was someone I met in a bar in New Orleans. Oh, she was an otter, a very eel in bed. She was also pregnant. I saw her through the abortion, through the yelling and screaming. Her nails tearing my hand. Her teeth working into my arm. Without my fucked-up goggles I could pick out the scars among the welding burns on my arm. The white marks hang before my eyes like a constellation. I know it well, the only one besides the Big and Little Dippers and the Pleiades. *Pleiades,* my father says and points. He isn't standing in the snow this time, although it is cold enough. His breath makes constellations of its own. He thumps his feet in slow alternation on the iron ground.

She chewed my arm. I chewed the end of my belt. We were companionable. We were sharing. It was the only thing we ever shared, and for twenty-five years I thought it was enough. *Sharing does it,* she said. *Agony does it.* How was I to know? It was in all the books.

But she was an otter. She was an eel. She raked my back with her nails. I thought that was love. I thought I owed her love in return. I left red marks on her neck. Oh, Lord, twenty-one. That's seven—seven-twelfths. Hang in there. It would have made a great memory, but it made no marriage at all.

I'll have to get new goggles so I can see her legs in the water. I want to see her legs in the water. For twenty-five years I wore my reading glasses everywhere so I wouldn't have to see anything, no legs, no tits, no asses. Now I want to see it all. But I can see so little I think I am smothering. She's somewhere in the water. Passing me. Meeting me. Coming back. Slipping by. An otter. An eel. She does her racing turn, somersaulting in the water, twisting, presenting her head in the new direction as if she were giving birth to herself. A long white tail like a comet. I am in the tail. It's neither water nor air. It's both at once and I don't know how to breathe it. I stand up, gasping, choking. Out of the water her head rises. The white storm of her wake catches up with her, swirls about us. Her head is all white bathing cap and black goggles. It rises a long way. She is very tall. An otter. An eel. Glistening. *Are you all right?* she says. *Are you all right?*

When the taxi turned my back on my mother, I was off to Chicago. I could forget about all that remembering. Wrong. I may have arrived in Chicago at last, but I never went through the process of getting there. All day I was on my way to Boston.

I left our little station, exactly as it was then. Red tile roof. Little porte cochere on the back. Just like something in a set of toy trains. Passed between the two Sand Cliffs, our forts, our sledding, our forbidden games. Over the Bridge— a glimpse of the Pond. And me fishing. At the Point. Off the Sand Dam. Off the Bridge itself, at the bottom of the abutment, fishing for shiners, soaking bread in my handkerchief, squeezing it back to dough. Catching pickerel before shiners, and shiners without bread. Sun and rain at once. Tall and short. Even blonde as in the oldest photographs. A medieval saint's life all at once on one surface, simultaneous as God's view of eternity.

I waited at the Junction and rattled over the Crossing already made famous by Saccovanzetti: the holdup, the murders, good men of Dedham and anarchist devils. And on the level floor of clouds over Lake Michigan, Mr. Mac-

Gregor's nursery burst into bloom. Neat rows of trees, straight and diagonal, splitting the vision, blinking open and shut, open and shut. Did I see Peter. Yes. And Flopsy, Mopsy, and Cottontail? Yes. Yes. And the South Station? Yes. And the Waiting Room? Yes. Even the very Bench to wait on under the sign Plymouth County? Yes. I sat there and waited while I went and cashed my ticket stub.

But at the same time, I went out of the Station. I stood in the sunlight, in the rain, and looked about me. I looked left and I looked right. There was a large black hole in the center of my vision. I didn't notice it. But I thought: the Hotel Essex. How convenient. How very convenient. I had once made a note of it—a permanent note—when I was having an affair. If we could both get to Boston, I had thought, how very convenient that would be. I stood in the rain, in the glare, and looked left and looked right and without looking at all slid the left and the right together and filled in the hole. The Station clock was striking slowly as if it had discovered an entirely new hour.

I went back to the pool on the Monday after Chicago. I wondered if the old man wondered about me when I was away. "Have a nice weekend?" he said.

"Yes," I said. "Very." I thought about it.

"That's nice," he said. "What light?" he said as the light flicked on in the pool.

"Through yonder window breaks," I said.

She had on her blue bathing suit. I'd know it anywhere, I said to myself as she walked toward the women's side.

"Very cold for this time of year," the old man said. He went past me to his lane. I eased myself into the water. The water was cold, too. I heard his flat crash as he hit the water. One thirty-sixth, I said. Coming and going we met. I checked him when I turned. I checked him in the water. He reclined on the water, arm reaching, knees bent. I reached and breathed. Reached and breathed. Twelve thirty-sixths—

one-third, I said. The swimming girl was in the water with me. She flashed past, trailing her great white tail. I saw him through it, glimmering like a saint on a wall. He reached. I reached. It was Michelangelo's *God Creating Adam*. I breathed and reached. The frenzy of bubbles was all about me. I reached. Smothered. Smothered and reached.

Billy Will's Song

Billy Will Jackson was in love with the world when he
got on the bus in Moline. He was singing his song—
"If this is all it is." Billy Will couldn't sing. Everyone told him so, but in his head he could hear the music,
and it was just as good as Elvis—better, because that mother was dead. And he was alive. And drunk.

He had had six beers while he was waiting for the bus.
"Hey, man," he said to the driver as he showed his ticket.
"Hey, man," he said to the old lady he stepped in front of to
get on the bus. "Hey, man," he said to the interior of the
bus in general. "If this is all it is," he sang. He started his
song shrill and went up from there. His voice climbed into
silence the way a siren sinks out.

Billy Will was a small man, but he dressed tough. He
wore Levis and boots and a white T-shirt with a pack of
cigarettes rolled up at the shoulder. On his left biceps he
had a tattoo. It was supposed to be a skull and crossbones,
but it turned out to be just a skull and only part of that. It
was as crude as if a child had done it with a ball-point pen
or he had done it himself one morning when he had a hangover. But it was a genuine tattoo, although it looked like a
death's head on a stone in a very old cemetery. On his left
forearm was a girl's name, Elva. He didn't know any Elva,
but he was glad to have the name even if it did look as if she
had done it herself when she was both drunk and very angry. In his left hand he carried his right arm.

The arm was brand-new. He had just got it in Moline, and he wasn't used to wearing it. It was shiny tan plastic with a gray glove over the curled fingers. He tapped the passengers on the shoulder with the gloved hand. "Hey, man," he said.

The doctors had tried to persuade him to have an arm with a metal hook on the end. Much more useful, they said. But he wanted an honest-to-God hand. That had some class. It was like the hand Mr. Shaw had when Billy Will was a kid. Mr. Shaw was principal of the high school. He had class—mainly the hand. Billy Will was going to tattoo H-O-L-D on the knuckles of his left hand and burn F-A-S-T into the knuckles of the glove like the sailors used to do. He knew what was what. He also knew that close behind him, oozing between the seats, was his three-hundred-pound wife, Norma Jean.

Norma Jean wasn't as drunk as Billy Will—she had had only four beers. She was watching her weight. She was glowering and unhappy. Billy Will didn't have to look around to see the expression on her face. "Hey, man," he said. "If this is all it is," he sang.

Norma Jean wasn't really three hundred pounds, but nobody would know it. She had passed two-fifty long ago and was well on her way, so she was as good as three hundred. The thing Billy Will loved best in all the world was to climb on her and go to sleep. She would lie very still—he would bite her if she moved. At least now he would lie lighter on her than ever. She had little enough as it was to complain of, and without the arm he was down to a hundred and ten.

The doctors joked with him at first and told him he'd have to watch his drinking because drunkenness went by body weight. The less you weighed, the less alcohol you needed to get drunk. That probably explained why Norma Jean never got really drunk, just moody. She'd be mean if she dared, but she didn't dare.

When he turned to let her get into the seat, he had to look at her. Her expression was exactly as he had imagined it. "You want a divorce?" he said. She didn't say say anything and heaved over to the window. She had to have a window. It was a good thing he liked to sit on the aisle where he could see things and relate to people.

The driver was already in his seat and was about to close the door when one last passenger got on, a man who was extreme in all possible ways. He was extremely large. He was extremely black. And he was as much a dude as it was possible to be. He wore pointy blue shoes and a blue suit that made Billy Will sick to his stomach. And he wore shades even in the shaded bus, the kind that look like silver and hide your eyes. Still, Billy Will was at peace with the world and held his arm up to the roof of the bus ready to give a high five. "Hey, man," he said.

The black man stopped in the aisle and seemed to consider Billy Will. "I got a longer reach," Billy Will said, "than Mohammed Ali. I can give you five while I'm sitting down. I got a longer reach than a gorilla."

The black man said nothing and showed nothing to indicate that he had come to any conclusion about Billy Will, but he brushed the arm aside and took the seat behind Billy Will and Norma Jean. "If this is all it is," Billy Will sang.

When the bus started at last, Norma Jean said, "Now maybe we can have a little peace and quiet."

"You want a divorce?" Billy Will said. He had been too easy on her in the past, but no more. He owed something to himself. It was a matter of class. He was a man who had lost an arm and had a lawsuit. The lawsuit had to do with his arm. The lawyer said he had a real good case. They'd sue for a million and settle for half. They had the company by the balls. Maybe sue the union too. The shop stewards knew all about the guards being off the machines. For once in his life it was going to be somebody else's ass for a change—a lot of somebodies. It was almost worth the arm—it *was* worth the arm *and* a leg to fix those bastards. Heads would roll. It was better than burning down the plant. They'd probably thank him for that. They'd get the insurance, and he'd be out of a job. Fixing them was worth an arm and a leg *and* his left ball. "If this is all it is," he sang.

"Honey," Norma Jean said as if she weighed ninety-eight pounds, "honey Billy Will, I'll bet everybody would like it if you'd just be a little quiet."

"You want a divorce?" Billy Will said.

"I know the driver would like it," she said exactly like her three-hundred-pound self. "I can see his eyes in the mirror."

Billy Will looked at the driver's eyes. They looked like the eyes of the doctors before they told him to watch his drinking. They looked like the eyes of the lawyer just after he said, "You got a real good case." "Hey, man," Billy Will said and waved his arm. The driver hooded his eyes.

"Gimme a cigarette, Norma Jean," Billy Will said. It stood to reason that even a tough guy couldn't get his cigarettes out of his sleeve with just one hand. You'd have to be double-jointed for that. But that's the way tough guys carried them. Billy Will had made a study. He had also seen that movie on TV where Spencer Tracy cleans out a bar full of bad guys. And Spencer Tracy only had one arm. He was a soldier from World War II, and he knew kung fu and like that and he was tough.

Norma Jean rolled the cigarettes out of his sleeve and shook one out for Billy Will. She also picked a wooden match out of the pack and gave him that too. Billy Will flicked the match with his thumbnail and lit the cigarette. The old lady across the aisle was admiring his cool. "Hey, man," he said.

"Would you mind not smoking?" she said. "I have asthma."

"It's a free country, lady," Billy Will said. "Even for a one-armed man. It's free for me to smoke, and it's free for you to have asthma." The old lady bit her lip and didn't say anything. She knew he had her there. She looked like an old maid schoolteacher who was used to having people say, Yes, ma'am, yes, Miss Burns—Miss Burns was his fourth-grade teacher. She rapped his knuckles to teach him manners, the old bag.

"Billy Will—" Norman Jean said.

"It's a free country for you too," Billy Will said. "You can have a divorce any time you want it. Only you won't be likely to find anybody to treat you like I do, anybody who's lost an arm and got a lawsuit."

Billy Will blew a jet of smoke toward the roof and watched it spread out and come curling down again. The old lady coughed. Billy Will felt very strong and very kind. He stood up. "You watch my arm, Norma Jean," he said kindly.

"Who'd want your old arm?" Norma Jean said.

"You watch it or you'll get it where you don't want it," Billy Will said.

As he turned toward the back of the bus he saw the black giant in the seat behind him. The silver glasses might have been looking at him or they might not. That's what he hated about those glasses. He was going to have to get himself a pair. "Hey, man," he said. The black man didn't say anything. He was probably asleep.

The sign on the door said: No Smoking in the Lavatory. Billy Will left the cigarette dangling from his lip—no one had to know he had practiced it in front of a mirror. The sign on the wall over the john was written with a felt-tip pen: This means you. But Billy Will knew it didn't.

Ever since that day in the emergency room, Billy Will knew he was special. When the doctor unwrapped his arm and said, "Shit," and whistled through his teeth, Billy Will knew it was bad. And when the nurse said, "Good luck," he knew he was a dead man. The last thing he saw was her eyes, her beautiful tired eyes over her surgical mask, and he knew that of all sad things she had ever seen, his—Billy Will's—death was the saddest.

And then he was awake again. It was as if he had been reborn. As if—yes—as if he had risen. He had been there and back and had seen that there was nothing to it. That's when he began to sing "If this is all it is." For a long time he sang it in his head because he couldn't make a sound, and he never noticed when his message began really to go out to the world, not that it mattered. He knew what he knew, and he was untouchable.

"Norma Jean," Billy Will said, once he was comfortable in his seat again, "I'll tell you something. It's hard to piss on a bus when you only have one hand. You can use your hand to hold your cock, so you flop around and piss on the walls and floor, or you can brace yourself against the wall and let you cock flop around so you piss all over yourself." Billy Will paused and admired his spotless pants and shoes. "Isn't that interesting? Norma Jean, I'm talking to you."

"No," Norma Jean said. She hadn't opened her eyes when he got into the seat, and she didn't open them now. Her mouth was already open, and she simply blew out the words when she had a breath going that way. It was as if a pumpkin head had spoken.

"Norma Jean," Billy Will said, "I think you're asking for a divorce. Here I tell you one of the interesting facts of the world and you don't even open your eyes." Norma Jean opened her eyes. She was the kind of woman who knew she could piss without any hands at all and couldn't see what all the fuss was about. She would never dream it would be easier to piss in the sink. Tough titty for Norma Jean if she ever needed what he could have told her. And if she went on like this and he gave up on her, there's no telling what she'd need.

"Norma Jean," he said, "I'm all you've got. I'm all that stands between you and the world. You got a husband who's been around. I lost an arm. I got a lawsuit. And I know what's what. You hear me?"

"I hear you," Norma Jean said without opening her eyes or using any muscles except the ones she absolutely needed to make a noise.

"Does that mean anything to you?"

"I feel it," Norma Jean said in just the same way.

Billy Will decided to accept that. There was no telling with Norma Jean. When they made love she would lie very quiet with her eyes closed and say, "Oh, Billy Will, I feel it so." But there was no sign of it that he could see. Her eyes didn't open. Her breathing didn't change. There wasn't a ripple in all her vast bulk. She could be having earthquakes, but none of it ever came to the surface. It was like dropping an atomic bomb down an old mine shaft.

Billy Will was disgusted with Norma Jean. That was his main reaction to her. Either he was disgusted or he was thinking about something else—his arm, his lawsuit, the St. Louis Cardinals, or horses. He could have been a rich jockey if anyone had told him there were still horses in the world. He had thought about being a cowboy, but his mother told him that was all old stuff and the only broncos cowboys used these days were four-wheel-drive pickups. He believed that. He saw it with his own eyes on TV. He might as well stay at home if that was all it was.

He looked around the bus benignly. His seat jolted as the man behind him levered himself into a new position with his knees. "Hey, man," Billy Will said in general.

Across the aisle, the old lady seemed to be examining her throat with a small flashlight. Billy Will focused his Hey, man. "I don't hear you coughing any," he said by way of congratulation.

The old lady took the flashlight out of her mouth—it

wasn't a flashlight. She gulped and gasped and said, "It's not like that."

"I know," Billy Will said. "My old man had it in the morning. He'd hawk and spit and no one went near him."

"It comes and goes," the old lady said. "The medicine helps." She held up the thing that wasn't a flashlight. "But it's mostly the Lord. The Lord giveth and the Lord taketh away."

"I used to think that," Billy Will said.

"You aren't one of those Commies, are you?" the old lady said. She pointed the former flashlight at him. It looked a little like a gun that an old lady might carry in her purse in these bad days.

Billy Will was shocked by the gun. It was getting so you couldn't trust anybody. But even more, he was shocked by the suggestion he might be one of those Commies. He almost said, "You want a divorce" but he remembered just in time that he wasn't married to her. He also remembered what you say to a little old lady with a gun. "Ma'am," he said as if she might rap his knuckles the next minute. He even advanced the gloved hand to accept the blow.

"Ma'am," he said, "if there's one thing I am it's a good American. That's for—for sure." He stumbled on the words because he remembered the ruler just when he was about to say "for shit sure."

"I'm one hundred percent American—well, I'm not a hundred percent anything anymore." He shrugged his empty sleeve at her. "But my new arm is better than ever. It's made right here in the U S of A with American material by Americans just as good as you and me."

The old lady sniffed. "Maybe you're a Moonie."

"No, ma'am," Billy Will said. For a moment he was speechless. It ought to be impossible for anybody not to see at a glance that he was a hundred percent in his right mind just as he could see she was a hundred percent old bag.

"Maybe you go around stealing our children," the old lady said.

"I don't want any children," Billy Will managed to say.

"And keeping them in com-munes and filling their poor heads with all kinds of atheistical un-American trash."

"I don't even have a com-mune," Billy Will whispered more to himself than to the old lady and more to the outraged universe than to himself.

"If you don't have a com-mune, how come you say you used to think that?"

Billy Will felt as if he had lost both arms and was standing in the lavatory of the rocketing bus trying to piss while being bounced from wall to wall. But if there was one thing he knew, it was what he thought. "Ma'am," he said. The gun was still lying in her lap, but she didn't seem to be paying much attention to it. Maybe he could clobber her with his arm if she started to get out of line. "Ma'am," he said. "I lost an arm. I suffered a lot. I learned a lot. I died and came back. I saw there's nothing to it."

"Nothing to it but the Lord," the old lady said fiercely. She stuck the gun in her mouth and pulled the trigger, but the gun didn't go off. She didn't even blink.

"And I thought there were no atheists in the foxholes," she said. "But the Lord will find you out. You can't have suffered like that for your country and come back without the help of the Lord. Will you pray with me?"

"No, ma'am," Billy Will said, still cautious in spite of the failure of the gun to blow the old lady's head off. "No, ma'am. I won't pray. There's nothing to pray."

"Then I must pray for you," the old lady said and shut up shop. She put the gun in her purse. She closed her eyes. She might have been praying for all Billy Will knew.

"If this is all it is," Billy Will sang. He fetched Norma Jean a clout with his elbow somewhere near her ribs. "Did you hear that?" he said.

"No," Norma Jean said without opening her eyes.

"She called me a Communist and an atheist and a loony—me. How do you like that?"

"Fine," Norma Jean said.

"What?" Billy Will said. "Woman, you must want a divorce."

"Awful," Norma Jean said, still without opening her eyes.

"Woman," Billy Will said, "pay attention.

"I am paying attention," Norma Jean said.

"Then open your eyes."

"I can pay attention with my eyes closed," Norma Jean said.

"When I close my eyes I go to sleep," Billy Will said. "Everybody does that. Now, open your eyes."

Norma Jean opened her eyes and rolled them slowly toward him as if each one weighed three hundred pounds.

"Now, Norma Jean," Billy Will said, "I've worked hard to keep you in the lap of luxury. Nothing but the best. Pizzas, Big Macs, lots of fries, ice cream—isn't that so?"

Norma Jean blinked ponderously, which passed for agreement in this particular catechism. It was what the magazine in the doctor's office called eye contact.

"I lost an arm for you. I got a lawsuit for you." Billy Will knew he was lying, but the old lady had knocked him off balance. He hadn't meant to lose his arm at all, not for anybody, and when he started the lawsuit, he thought only of becoming a rich jockey who had lost his arm in a race. What it would mean to Norma Jean never entered his mind. "We'll be rich," he said. "We won't even have to go out to get pizza and fries and ice cream. Whatever we want we'll order off. The sky's the limit in the lap of luxury."

Norma Jean didn't open her eyes. Billy Will couldn't even tell if she was breathing—what lungs ever made by God could move that lard? One of these days he was going to wake up and find out that she had forgotten to breathe in the middle of the night.

"Norma Jean, do you hear me?"

Norma Jean rolled up her lids. Her eyes were exactly where she had left them, eyeball to eyeball with his. "I hear you, Billy Will," she said.

"Woman, I'm offering you the world."

Norma Jean closed her eyes. "Thank you, Billy Will," she said.

Billy Will suddenly knew that her eyes were staring at him from behind her lids, that she could see him perfectly. He also knew it was time for him to assert himself.

"Or I'm taking it back," he said. He made a sweep with his real hand as if he were raking in all the chips.

"Yes, Billy Will," she said.

"Do you want a divorce?"

"No, Billy Will," she said.

"Then what do you want with all this craziness?"

She hung fire for a moment. "I want you to go back to work," she said. Her eyes were open now. She was still looking at him, but her eyes moved and blinked like a real person's. They even glistened a little as if with real tears. Now he hung fire.

"You know they want you back," she said.

"I'm a good man," Billy Will said. "But I lost an arm and got a lawsuit."

"Forget that stuff, Billy Will, honey," Norma Jean said. "Go back to work."

But Billy Will knew what he owed to himself. She had shaken him there for a moment, but now he remembered. "There's just some things you can't understand, Norma Jean, honey," he said, "what a man has to do."

Norma Jean closed her eyes and turned her face to the window. Billy Will looked out at the endless fields of corn and beans, at the remote houses in their clumps of trees, at all the green and working world. He imagined Norma Jean studying that through her eyelids, but then he realized that what she was seeing was his reflection in the window.

"Norma Jean," he said, "you piss me off. I'm all you've got, and you're nothing but one of those air mattresses and you aren't even comfortable to sleep on." He knew he was lying, and he even knew that she knew it, but a fight is a fight. Norma Jean didn't stir. This might be the time she had forgotten to breathe. He poked her—at least she wasn't cold yet.

"Before God I didn't do it on purpose," Billy Will said, forgetting for the moment that he was now an atheist. "A man would have to be crazy to do a thing like that on purpose. I saw the machines chew up my old man's fingers. I saw a woman snatched baldheaded, scalped as clean as any Indian. I'd have to be crazy even if I didn't know what it was really like until it was me. Norma Jean, you don't know how it hurt."

Norma Jean still didn't stir, but she said to the window, "I never said you stuck your arm in that machine on purpose."

"Hush," Billy Will said, "everybody thinks I lost it in Vietnam."

Billy Will had a sense of an earthquake behind him. He felt doom coming upon him. A huge blue cloud hung over him, and a voice spoke out of the cloud. The enormous shining eyes of the cloud froze him. "Shut your fucking mouth," the cloud said. "I'm sick of you and your bitching. I just about lost my eyes in Vietnam, and I don't want to hear another word out of you."

The cloud receded. The hush after the storm spread through the bus as if a curse of silence had been laid on it. All the way into Peoria, Billy Will sat and listened to his own breathing. He listened to the familiar sound of Norma Jean's sleep. But there was nothing else.

At the Peoria station the driver jumped out first. The passengers started to follow. The vast black man stood in the aisle and held everyone up while the old lady gathered her parcels and her purse and her little gun. Then she got off. The black man got off. When there was no one else left, Billy Will said, "Let's go, Norma Jean." He stood up and started toward the door. "If this is all it is," he sang. Norma Jean oozed behind him with his arm slung over her shoulder like a gun.

Visiting the Dead

J
ust after sunset three little green herons flew into a dead tree far out in the swamp. There was still enough light for binoculars to make sure of them. A mallard flew over, and then another. A kingfisher dropped from a bare branch, flew low over the water, shrieking, and rose sharply to a new vantage point farther away, almost out of sight. A redheaded woodpecker darted from tree to tree. After such a day, birds were the only thing.

It began when Logan looked at the calendar and said, "Today is the day." He groaned. One of the best things about living alone again after all those years was being free to groan. If his shoulder hurt after a hard night's sleep, he groaned. If his back refused to straighten after he bent, he groaned. If his knees ached on the stairs, he groaned. He groaned often from sheer oppression of spirit. He had a lifetime of suppressed groans well saved and ready for use.

He put on his glasses and looked again at his calendar, although he knew very well what he would see—OLD LADY DAY—blocking the whole of his private Saturday.

He was unwashed and unshaved. He had got as far as his coffee. He had, so to speak, set it before himself on the kitchen table and was zeroing in on the heat when he remembered. He groaned again. "Jesus," he said.

He lifted the cup with both hands. The accustomed shock

alerted him. He glanced quickly over the rim of his cup. There was no one to hear him.

Of course it didn't begin then. Nothing ever begins just then. He could trace it back to his birth, to his mother's birth, the biological clock set ticking and counting down. Born astride the grave, as the Greeks put it.

Actually there were two old ladies, Logan's aunts, his mother's sisters. They lived together to share expenses and loneliness and confusion. But most of all they protected their capital for a rainy day. For *rainy day* read *rest home.*

Of course he had no one to blame but himself. He didn't know what had possessed him to call the old ladies and promise to come down and take them for a drive. Actually he hadn't thought of the old ladies for years, hadn't seen them since his mother's funeral. As far as he could remember, he hadn't visited them since he used to come down to drive his mother on her rounds, and it would never have occurred to him that they would want to make a tour to their old houses and their ancestral graves.

"I'll do it," Logan had said.

"You're all we've got," Aunt Jane had said.

"You're our heir," Aunt Elizabeth had said.

Logan was inclined to laugh at the idea of an inheritance. There had never been any money in his family—enough to bury people on. He used to claim that the family motto was: Everyone pays for his own funeral. And yet, in another part of his mind, he knew there was money. All his life it had been drifting toward him death by death, a little here, a little there, funneling toward the old ladies and then to him. He used to say when he was younger, "I'll become a Catholic again and pray for their happy death or speedy recovery."

He knew they would go fast when they went. His people didn't fool around. But he also knew they would probably live to be a hundred and fifty and bury him and all his generation. It wasn't just the inheritance anyway. More than an inheritance went into a birthright.

He groaned in spirit and began to prepare himself. The old ladies were to supply lunch so he laid in a supply of Gelusil. There was no telling what they would expect him to eat. The morning after his mother's funeral they had offered him pie out of dim and hopeful memories of what a man would eat for breakfast. He had not been able to disappoint them, and he had suffered indigestion all the way home. The mere memory produced a burp. However, if all went well he should be able to get to the swamp for the birds' last flurry of the day and for the beginning of night.

As the light faded, one of the three green herons flew down and out of sight. Frogs croaked in the swamp. Tree frogs sang in the forest. A bat staggered over all the visible sky. Nighthawks, circling high in the air, flew by the radar of their regular squawks. Among the lily pads at his feet, something stirred the water. He never saw what it was.

The old ladies had the table set and were ready to thank God for their pious nephew. They also had on their good dresses, the ones they always wore to watch Dr. Baker on TV on Sunday mornings. They even had their hats laid ready on the desk near the door. Logan had never seen the hats. However, they were proper old-lady hats and must have gone in and out of style a dozen times since they were bought—if indeed old-lady hats ever do go out of style any more than their wearers. But, in style or out, the hats did more than anything else to convince Logan that this was really an important day.

Tenderly, very tenderly, he installed Aunt Jane in the backseat of his car and Aunt Elizabeth in front. Aunt Elizabeth was the less mobile of the two, and the backseat of his car was not really roomy. Carefully he tucked afghans around the old ladies' legs. "There you are, Aunt Elizabeth," he said. "There you are, Aunt Jane."

Logan could hear himself telling the story at cocktail parties and dinners all winter long. "Jesus Christ," he would say, "I tucked them up and looked at my watch. 'Drive like hell,' I said to myself. Anybody knows that with old ladies you have about two hours before you have to find a bathroom—and if you don't, tough luck. The afghans become soakers and the car begins to smell like the French Quarter on Sunday morning."

"I don't recognize that house," Aunt Elizabeth said. It was the first thing she had said on the trip, although she sat up very straight and looked about her, bright and alert like an idiot child sitting up in bed.

They had stopped at the first shrine on the pilgrimage. Logan wasn't sure he recognized it either. He had been expecting a shabby old house, dingy, in need of paint, a brick or two out of the chimney. Instead, the house was dazzling white and the chimney was impeccable. In a more wide-awake town, the owner would have signed the date in the lower right-hand corner: 1795, 1810, c. 1812.

"Silly," Aunt Jane said, "that's your very own house where you lived for all those years before you came to me."

Logan studied it curiously. It was Aunt Elizabeth's house all right. It couldn't be anything else, even if all his life it had been falling apart, always threatening to go too far. He wasn't sure he had visited the house as a child—not unless that was where he was expected to play with the ritual cast-iron toys, the indestructible bequest of many childhoods. Unless that was where he had been shown the child's chair that had belonged to his mother—in her turn—and that she had pushed before her upside down, wearing the round posts flat. Unless he dreamed the fire engines and the chair.

He wished he had come sooner so that he could be past this by now, but it hadn't been easy to arrange. One or the other of the old ladies was always ailing and miraculously recovering, so the promised tour was constantly postponed.

"Someone was always dying," Aunt Jane said at lunch.

"Someone was always in the spare room waiting to die," Aunt Elizabeth said.

"Hiding under the bed—"

"—white hair among the dust balls—"

"—or taking strange names—"

"—wearing Halloween masks."

"The house was always hushed," Aunt Jane said.

"We were ashamed to laugh."

"For our friends, the quiet was as good as a haunted house, but safer. They liked to sleep over sometimes. They liked to whisper all night, thinking someone might be dead in the next room—or dying—or about to shriek. They thought it was crazy, and they loved it. I thought it was crazy, and I did not love it."

"I never got used to the shrieks," Aunt Elizabeth said.

"I never got used to the bolster muffled up in the bed and the fugitive under the bed," Aunt Jane said. "I never got used to wondering and fearing and hoping that this time it would be a corpse we pulled out from under the bed—but there was always another one ready to come and die."

"We were never able to bury them all," Aunt Elizabeth said.

Logan found all this fabulous. Nobody had ever died on his hands. His grandfather, to be sure, had died in his own house and was decently laid out there. His own father, however, was not laid out at home, but at the grandfather's house. Logan as a boy paid them formal visits, both at the house and the cemetery.

Those were the only times he went to the cemetery as a child except for the ritual occasions of Memorial Day, Armistice Day, and the Fourth of July when he followed the parade to hear the soldiers shoot. It was the old cemetery they marched to then and fired their ragged volleys over the graves bright with little flags, spring flowers, and autumn leaves. Afterward the boys would scramble for the ejected shells, bright brass gleaming among the leaves. And the old men in blue would be driven away in cars, and the not-quite-so-old men from the Spanish war would walk, and the soldiers would march, out of step, their rifles askew, their uniforms ill-fitting and old, made long ago for someone else.

"I've got one," Logan says. He has found it against a gravestone, under a little flag. The metal is still warm as he holds it in his hand, kneeling, eye to eye with the Minuteman on the flag-holder.

In Mallorca the dead are stacked in filing cabinets, a long wall of cabinets above ground, long winding alleys of cabinets below ground. There are flowers everywhere and candles, for it is the Day of the Dead. The walks are thronged with people. Almost the only undecorated file drawer belongs to an expatriate American couple. Logan steals a flower for them from a nearby drawer. After this, well pleased, he goes to the racetrack next door and cautiously loses a hundred pesetas.

The first cemetery was Aunt Jane's. She was to be buried with her husband's family, but her sister, who had never married, was to be buried with their father and mother— Logan's own grandfather and grandmother, he forced himself to remember. This cemetery was small. It almost looked like a mistake, a lot in a residential area, although probably it was there first and the houses grew up around it. Logan tried to check this hypothesis by comparing gravestones with probable building dates: both c. 1910.

"Where is our stone?" Aunt Jane said.

"Straight on," Logan said, "a little farther back." He had Aunt Jane on one arm and Aunt Elizabeth on the other, leading them slowly over the uneven ground.

"Here are the Allens," Aunt Elizabeth said. "Jane, do you remember how bad Ruth Allen was in school?"

"Oh, yes, indeed," Aunt Jane said. Both of them laughed.

"What did she do bad?" Logan asked just to say something.

"Oh, she was very bad," Aunt Jane said.

"She was a very bad girl," Aunt Elizabeth said.

"Here are the Watsons," Aunt Jane said. "Can you see what it says on that stone over there?"

"Bates," Logan said. "Henry Bates."

"Oh, that old fool," Aunt Elizabeth said.

"It was bad enough in life having him for a neighbor," Aunt Jane said. "How about that stone?"

"Fisher," Logan said. "Edward Fisher." He was a little embarrassed because he knew he was just testing to see if Aunt Jane remembered her husband's name.

"She's so old she can just about remember her own name," Logan would say. "It's no wonder she didn't recognize the stone or her husband's name. She had to spell out *Jane, beloved wife,* before she knew where she was."

At Primo's mother's wake, men and women alike weep and call, "Mama, Mama." Primo's mother herself looks as if she were made up to do a commercial. Logan expects her to sit up and try to sell him pasta.

At Red Murphy's wake—both these wakes are in the same night, after the store has closed, around midnight, and they are the only ones Logan has ever attended. It is the summer after his sophomore year. Red drowned on his day off for no reason whatever, and at this wake the women weep and the men clench their teeth, showing clearly that they have shaved too close. They look skinned. Red looks silly. He isn't like that at all. He doesn't try to pinch the girls, and he doesn't say *shit* even once. In the kitchen old men play cards. They whack their cards on the table and salt their beer to ward off evil spirits.

A flock of pigeons sprang up from an island in the swamp, banked sharply and disappeared in midair, reappeared again farther on. A banner of blackbirds flung across the sky. A great blue heron croaked twice but remained hidden.

"So there we are," Aunt Jane said. "There we are. There is my place. And there's a place for you, Edward. We always wanted you with us."

"Where?" Logan said.

"On the other side of your uncle."

"Oh, what a bad girl she was," Aunt Elizabeth said.

"There's plenty of room," Aunt Jane said.

"And there's room for both of us," Logan's sister says.

They are standing in the snow at their parents' grave. Theirs are the only footprints in the whole vast cemetery— except for rabbits and birds. It is New Year's Day, the anniversary of their father's death and very nearly of their mother's as well, forty years later. This is the first time they have visited the graves together, although his mother and sister have made the pilgrimage together every year for forty years.

"There's room enough for both of us," his sister says. The tears freeze on her cheeks. The wind is bitter and the unmarked snow lies all about them.

Logan is recently divorced and has come home because he feels at the moment that his sister is all he has. Even so, he knows there will be someone. He feels entitled to some good luck.

At the dig in London, skulls come out of the ground like potatoes. There is no accounting for them. Some say a plague pit, but clearly, in that case, there would be more than just skulls.

To be sure, the site—a Roman bath—has lain under an eighteenth-century churchyard, the church long since blown away by the Germans, but the graves have all been excavated with due care and ceremony by professionals in that line of work. The site has been surrounded by cloth stretched on poles so tall that even from the top of a double-decker bus no one can catch an unhallowed glimpse of hallowed bones. The site has been pronounced clear before it is surrendered to the archeologists.

But still the skulls come out of the ground. "Quick," the site supervisor says, "bury them in the spoils heap or we'll be held up forever while they're being dated." It is a fact of English life that skulls dated before 597 (the year of St. Augustine's mission to the Saxons) are potatoes, but skulls after that date must be ritually handled by professionals in that line of work.

" 'Quick, pour the cement,' the highway construction boss said, 'before anyone sees that mosaic, or we'll be held up while the archeologists diddle about.' " It is at another dig, the one at Heathrow, that a construction worker tells Logan that story.

Logan always wonders why he never put one of the skulls in his knapsack.

"And here are the Masons, our cousins," Aunt Jane said.
"She *would* marry that man," Aunt Elizabeth said.
"No one could ever tell her a thing," Aunt Jane said.
They had all crept back to the gravel path dividing the cemetery in half. Aunt Elizabeth leaned less and less heavily on Logan's arm and now seemed almost to be pulling him along.

"There are the Lightfoots," Aunt Elizabeth said. They all stopped.

"These are different Lightfoots," Aunt Jane said. "Those Lightfoots buried in Easton."

"No," Aunt Elizabeth said, "her mother was Emily and her father was Walter, and there they both are."

"Then where is she?" Aunt Jane said. "She was buried with them."

"No, Jane, no," Aunt Elizabeth said. "She was buried in New Hampshire with her husband's folks."

"Oh, my," Aunt Jane said. "I'm all confused."

"She was my special friend," Aunt Elizabeth said.

"They really came alive in the cemeteries," Logan would say. "They knew everybody. Who married who and who was whose second cousin once removed. Except nobody had any names. They were all he or she, and the two of them knew exactly who they were talking about every time. They could have ten *he*'s and fifteen *she*'s going at the same time and never miss a beat. But they couldn't remember my name. They called me Edward. And they called me William. They even called me Alice. And the only time they called me Paul they were thinking of another Paul."

It was nearly night now. The last light had all but faded from the sky. A star shone faintly. And then another. A largish bird, perhaps a duck, flew at treetop level along the edge of the swamp, directly overhead, and lit in a large tree a little farther on. Logan could barely make it out against the darkness of the trunk.

"It can't be a duck," he said. He had never seen a duck in a tree. "But it can't be anything else," he said.

He tried his binoculars, but they didn't help much. The bird seemed to be streaked about the head, but it was too dark to be sure even of that.

Logan found his way back through town. Turn left. Turn right. Stop.

"Why are we stopping here?" Aunt Jane said.

"It's your house," Aunt Elizabeth said.

"It is not," Aunt Jane said.

"It's your very own house, Jane, where you and Edward lived for forty years," Aunt Elizabeth said.

"It's your house, Aunt Jane," Logan said.

"Then what's that house there?" Aunt Jane pointed to the house next door.

"That's Aunt Martha's and Uncle Philip's house, Aunt Jane," Logan said.

"His sister Martha lived there," Aunt Elizabeth said, speaking to invisible witnesses. "She was sickly."

Logan knows about Aunt Martha's sickliness. "Poor soul," he says. He doesn't know why he says that. He just knows that when you say Martha, you say, Poor soul. It is her unheroic epithet. She would have lived forever if she hadn't taken it into her head to die—the only manipulation she hadn't tried yet. His own mother learned everything she knew from Aunt Martha. And Aunt Martha stayed in bed all her life—it was like a Gothic novel. His mother made it through nine months while she was having him, but after that she got up, although not very far. She had her little man to look after her. And it only took him four years of analysis to know all this.

"It's your house, all right, Aunt Jane," Logan said.

"It doesn't look right," Aunt Jane said.

"It's your house, Jane," Aunt Elizabeth said.

"It was never red," Aunt Jane said.

"It's been painted," Logan said. And indeed it had, complete with the date in the lower right-hand corner, 1799.

"It was white with green shutters," Aunt Jane said.

"See how they fixed the garage," Logan said. "And the summerhouse looks better than ever."

"Who's that man?" Aunt Jane said.

The man had come out of the house and was clipping the neat hedge, standing so that he could keep Logan's car under surveillance.

"He must be the owner," Logan said. The man was every inch an owner, from his bald and shining head to his pristine Adidas.

"He's taking good care of the place, Aunt Jane," Logan said.

There was a time, when Logan first realized he wouldn't be a child forever, when he used to imagine coming back to the old house. He sat in the window seat and looked out, absently half opening and closing the folding shutters. He looked through the miraculous writing in the glass, the elegant diamond flourishes, C L N, 1803. He saw himself as a man get out of a car parked across the street. He came to the front door. He rang the bell. "I used to live here," he said. He closed the shutters entirely.

The old part of Highgate Cemetery has been lost in the jungle for centuries. When Logan walks there he is in Cambodia, in the Yucatan. He forces his way through the undergrowth. He scratches his arms on real thorns and on wrought-iron imitations. He slips on moss-covered marble. He discovers tombs rich in guano. Marble gleams through the greenery. Vines overturn the marble. In the midst of this desolation he finds a woman stretched on the ground, weeping over a fresh grave.

The Mason family had originally been farmers, and their plot was out in the country. Logan knew the way vaguely once he had determined that the cemetery and the old Mason place were not far apart. The road was winding and narrow and looked much as he remembered it except that for the first mile or so a thin border of new houses straggled out from the town, and there were no dairy cattle in the rocky fields, only a few horses, here and there an abandoned car. Then they came to the pine woods, edged with ruined stone walls and divided mysteriously by more walls running off among the trees.

"It must have been like this when you were girls," Logan said.

"Oh, no," Aunt Jane said. "These were fields."

"Those on the right were ours," Aunt Elizabeth said.

"There was wheat at first," Aunt Jane said. "And then cows. And then our father just gave up and went to work in the mill. And the woods sprang up."

"He cut off his fingers in the mill," Aunt Elizabeth said. She held up her right hand and slashed her left forefinger across it. "Three of them. He used to thump us on the head with the stumps when we were bad. It really hurt."

"Oh, how it hurt," Aunt Jane said. They both laughed.

"Were you as bad as—as Ruth Allen?" Logan said.

"Oh, wasn't she bad?" Aunt Elizabeth said.

"She was very bad," Aunt Jane said.

After the woods came the cranberry bogs, dark winy red as the season wore on. And in the midst of the bogs on a little hill in an oak grove was the cemetery.

The bird that was certainly a duck and was certainly not a duck flew from its tree and crossed the swamp to another tree. It was too far away now to be picked out at all. The light was too bad.

"That's got to be a duck," he said aloud, but he didn't see how it could be. Still, the name *wood duck* came to mind, and he wondered if wood ducks roost in trees.

The cemetery was beautifully isolated, nothing but sky and empty bogs all around. At the bottom of a short slope a stream ran through its winding avenue of trees and emptied into the bog reservoir. Bright leaves rustled underfoot, and dull brown leaves rattled on the trees.

"Father and Mother," Aunt Elizabeth said.

"And Paul, who died in the war," Aunt Jane said.

"Uncle William."

"And Mary, who never grew up."

"Evelyn Nelson—"

"Hush."

"The three babies."

"Our brothers."

"And my very own place," Aunt Elizabeth said. She left Logan's side and stepped into the plot as if she were about to walk into the earth as into a pond. She turned. "There's lots of room, William. We'd be glad to have you."

"Thank you," Logan said. In his confusion he stooped and picked up a shotgun shell from the base of a stone. He closed his hand over the bright red of the shell, over the brass of the base. The metal was warm from the sun. He could do worse than lie in a place where hunters come.

"You've come back to us," Aunt Elizabeth said.

"You should make plans," Aunt Jane said. "You should always make plans."

"Oh, the poor souls," Logan would say.

The mysterious bird flew darkly back across the swamp. It was coming toward him now and much lower—perhaps twenty feet above the water. And at the near edge of the swamp it vanished. It had seemed to fly straight at a tall dead stub of a tree, white and ghastly in the night, but it must have veered at the last moment and flown on into the woods. He studied a small round hole high up in the stub at exactly the place where the bird had seemed to disappear. He couldn't imagine the bird flying at full speed into that tiny hole. It must have flown past—or not. This was all very mysterious.

Previous Winners of

David Walton, *Evening Out*
Leigh Allison Wilson, *From the Bottom Up*
Sandra Thompson, *Close-Ups*
Susan Neville, *The Invention of Flight*
François Camoin, *Why Men Are Afraid of Women*
Mary Hood, *How Far She Went*
Molly Giles, *Rough Translations*